SAFFRON

AND

SECRETS

SHARON WOODS

For all the grandma's who leave us with sweet memories and warm hugs...

Jonathan

I never thought I'd see the day I'd be walking into a florist shop to buy a bouquet of flowers. But here I am...

"I'm here now. I'll deliver them to her soon and get back to pick you up and take you to your meeting," I say into my phone to my boss.

He sighs. "All right, call me when you're downstairs."

I hang up and tuck my phone back into my pants.

I've been assigned to do this for my good friend and now boss, James. He's head over heels for a girl named Abigail and he's sent me to buy flowers and personally deliver them to her. I can't exactly argue with him when he's paying me to do this.

The windows of the shop are full of colorful plants. Some are hanging from the ceiling in baskets and many others are in pots on the floor. Dread hits me. I'd rather pick up dry cleaning than do this. They aren't even for me, so why didn't I try to convince him to order them online and have them delivered?

Oh, that's right. He wouldn't. He wanted her to feel special and have someone she knows deliver them. He wants that personal touch. *Insert my eye roll and hand me a bucket to puke in.*

I roll my shoulders back and take a deep breath, convincing myself I can do this. It's just a flower shop. The quicker I get inside the store, the quicker I can get out. I step inside and a chime above the door sounds. Sally's florist is enormous, and they sell way more than just flowers. There is artwork all over the walls for sale and candles laid out on every surface. Even furniture has tags, meaning they are for sale too.

As I walk further into the shop, I find more furniture accessories scattered around. This place is just too big; I am trying to find someone who works here. I want to pick up my boss's order and be done with it.

I peer around at all the flowers. Who knew there would be so many types in a rainbow of colors? I've never been much of a flower guy myself. I know of red and white roses and that's it. I'm not someone who buys flowers. I've always been a one-night stand kind of guy. I've spent my entire adult life creating an app called Integration Software and then helping my parents' business until we had an argument and I left.

I notice a blonde florist working behind the counter and quicken my pace. However, as I reach her, the phone rings. Fuck! I pause and rub my head while she answers it.

"Hello, thank you for calling Cygnature Blooms, where bigger is always better. May I take your order, please?"

I put my hands in my suit pockets to stop myself from fidgeting. I hate being in a place like this. I can't wait to leave.

After a couple more minutes, she hangs up. I step closer to the counter, not wanting to waste another second.

She smiles at me politely. "Sorry, sir, I have to serve this customer first. She was before you. She just had to answer a call. I'll be back to help you soon."

"Sure," I say with a tight smile.

I watch her move to the opposite wall and assist a black-haired woman. I move around, needing to do something, so there's no harm in wasting time looking around. My eyes flick to them every now and again to watch their exchange, hoping she won't take much longer. They walk to the counter, and I almost fist-pump the air.

"The saffron seems low today," the black-haired woman remarks in a soft tone.

"Yes, there wasn't much available this week..." the florist says, and I zone out. I stopped listening to their conversation when I ran my gaze over the back of the black-haired woman. As I stand directly behind her, I can't help but appreciate her hourglass shape and heart-shaped ass in her black pants and white top. The woman turns to leave, and I suck in a sharp breath. I'm totally taken aback. She not only has a great body, but her face is impeccable—her full lips are pink and pouty, while her green eyes glimmer under the lights.

And when she smiles, my breath hitches.

I change my mind in that instant. Maybe I should come to these places more often if people like her come here. Like an idiot, I stand there, slack-jawed, unable to move, until she dips her head and walks past, holding her flowers. Her sweet scent hits my nostrils, and I sniff deeper to take it in. It's sweet like honey with a floral touch.

I clear my throat and step forward.

"I'm here to pick up a bouquet," I say.

"Sure. Name?"

"James White."

"Oh yes, I'll grab it now," the receptionist says with a broad smile.

After collecting the bouquet, I step outside and text James.

Jonathan: I got it, boss. I'll drop them off now.

As soon as I read his text back, my phone flashes in my hand, and I squeeze it slightly and curse under my breath. *Fuck off.*

I grind my teeth, annoyed, and hit decline on my mother's incoming call. Unwilling to deal with her right now, I stuff my phone into my pocket. I'd rather deliver fucking flowers.

RUBY

I'M PICKING UP MY weekly saffron order to take to my grandma Flora's. The familiarity of the city lets me zone out and listen to all the hustle and bustle around me. Everyone else is going about their day on a Friday, but I can take today off and work Monday to Thursday and Saturday instead. This routine allows me to spend time with her. She isn't getting any younger at eighty-three, after all. Besides my parents, she is my world. I share everything about my life with her.

The chime goes off, and my lips curve into a smile when the smell of flowers hits me. It makes me happy being in here. If flowers aren't your thing, we can't be friends. They're so beautiful and can make your darkest days turn brighter. When you're sad, you buy flowers, and when you're happy, you buy them too. There isn't any occasion or emotion where you wouldn't.

I walk over to where the saffron is kept. My shoulders hunch when I see a low stock. We look forward to pie baking every Friday. It's our thing. I try not to think about what will happen when she goes. No, I don't dare think what that would mean. I push that thought away and pick up a small bunch.

As I'm about to turn, I hear Sally, the owner of the florist shop, say, "Morning, Ruby."

I spin and offer a warm smile. "Good morning, Sally."

She wouldn't ask me if I would like another flower; I've been coming here way too long for that. She knows I'm here for my saffron, and that's all. Instead, we make small talk about other things.

"How's Flora?" Sally wears her blonde hair in a neat bun and a black apron covers her jeans and top. She's in her late thirties and started this business when she had kids. I love how kids didn't stop her from chasing her dreams.

"She's good. Opinionated as ever, but that's what we love about her."

"She still trying to get you to settle down and get married?"

Giggling, I hand the saffron to Sally.

"Every week, without doubt. She asks if I'm dating or if I'm talking to anyone. To which she gets the same answer, *No, I'm busy working.*"

She tilts her head to indicate we walk to the front of the store so she can wrap the bouquet and continue our conversation.

"I think she wants to know you're happy and that you don't work too much."

I sigh. "That's exactly what she thinks. I'll miss my chance to get married or have kids because all I do is work, but I love it."

She wraps the bunch up, and I swipe my card to pay.

"It's so important to love your job. I get it. Just don't forget to have a little fun too." She wiggles her brows as she passes me the wrapped flowers.

I chuckle with a small eye roll and say, "I'm leaving before you get as bad as her."

She smirks and waves, and as I turn, I'm met with large brown eyes that I've seen here before. Which is a nice surprise. He stands out in his black suit, defined jawline, five o'clock shadow, dark brown—*or is it black?*—wavy hair. I feel a flush hitting my cheeks. How much did he hear? Hopefully, not too much, because that would be embarrassing. I don't need the world knowing I'm on a dry spell and haven't been on a date in over twelve months.

Locking gazes with him causes a flutter in my stomach...a new and exciting feeling, but I need to get a grip. This guy is taken, for sure. He's in a florist shop, so obviously he must have a girlfriend. He looks to be in his thirties so he could even have a wife and kids, and I'm drooling over him.

He offers a panty-melting smile, and I almost melt into a puddle. Damn, he's my dream man. There's a kindness in his smile that makes me want to talk to him, but I bet if I spent time with him, I'd find out he has multiple girlfriends and is on countless dating apps.

Why is he wearing that suit?

Where is my intelligent brain? I seem to have lost it the moment I saw him. No wonder Sally was wiggling her brows...she was hinting at him.

Oh God, how cringy.

I smile and dip my head, clutching my flowers to my chest. As I pass by him, I get a whiff of his delicious scent—a mix of caramel and spice. I want to bathe in it. Ignoring the tingling feeling, I walk out, keeping my gaze focused on the exit. When the outside air hits me, I take a deep breath and continue to my car, but something feels off.

I look over my shoulder but see nothing unusual, and after a quick scan around, nothing seems out of place. But the strange feeling doesn't leave me, and after discovering a note yesterday on my car that said, *I miss you*. I can't shake the eerie feeling, so I walk faster on the concrete and my breaths quicken as a slight panic hits. Something is definitely off. Maybe I should have stayed and talked to the handsome man. We would have walked the same direction. He definitely felt like he could protect me.

Jonathan

I'M OUT OF THE shop, holding the large arrangement for Abigail. The flowers today differ from the ones last week. This weeks are nice except for the obnoxious white flowers sticking up so high. They're hitting me in the face and pissing me off. And the smell is so strong I've felt my eyes tingle, my throat swell, and whatever the fuck these are, I'm going to insist he never orders them again. Otherwise, I'm paying for delivery personally.

As soon as I get in the car, I pull out my phone to text him.

Jonathan: Don't buy these flowers again unless you want her to break up with you.

James: Why? What's wrong with them?

Jonathan: **They're making me feel odd, like I'm having an allergic reaction.**

James: *(laughing emoji)* **Are you serious? What do they look like? Can you go back in and change them?**

I furiously type back, ignoring my itchy eyes and throat.

Jonathan: **Hell no! I'm not going back in. I don't have time. I need to drop these off unless you want me to organize a delivery?**

James: **No, you need to take them. It's okay. I just won't order lilies again.**

Jonathan: **I don't even want to know why you know the name of these god-awful flowers.**

**James: It's called love, John, and the day
you find it, you'll know this shit matters
to them. And *you* will do anything to put
a smile on their face and make them feel
special.**

I scoff. That will never happen. He should know that.

**Jonathan: I'll take your word for it. I'll
text you when I'm back at the office.**

I drop the phone down to the front seat and drive out
of the parking spot. As I do, I blink rapidly spotting *her*.
Those luscious hips move in tight jeans and wavy dark
hair flowing in the breeze. I slow the car and smile as I
see she's holding her saffron flowers, and walking slightly
faster compared to other people around her.

I frown and wonder if she's late for something. Work?
Maybe a partner?

Someone as pretty as her would be taken.

As I pass her, I can't help but move my gaze to the
rearview mirror, trying to get one final glimpse of her.
When she is out of my sight, I concentrate on the road

ahead as James's words replay. What would it feel like to want to do all that sappy shit for a woman?

I shake off the ridiculous thought. I can't even imagine it.

I'm back staring at the mirror when my phone rings. Tearing my gaze down to the screen, I groan at my mother's name, and I don't even hesitate when I hit the decline button. After I drop the flowers off to Abigail and get back in the car, I see a text from her.

Mom: Please call me.

I brush off her text because I don't have time to speak to her right now. I have to quickly pick up James and take him to a meeting. But I know I can't avoid her forever. We may have disagreed about *my* future, but they aren't bad parents. They need to let me choose my path, not dictate every step of my life.

I'm not rebelling; I'm too old for that shit, but I don't think money means you can tell me what to do. Hence why I got a job even when I have money—a lot of it and not just family money.

But working is something I enjoy doing, and being friends with James since I was young has meant I could help him and he understands me. I can open up to him and work for him without judgment.

After taking James to the meeting, I decide to call Mom back. Having it hanging over my head will not help me sleep tonight. Even if I train or have drinks with friends, I'll still be wondering what she wanted.

I sit in the car with my eyes closed and the back of my head lying on the headrest as I try to calm my body and mind before I call her. When I'm ready, I sit up. *Here goes nothing…*

"There you are. Why are you avoiding me?" she rushes out angrily.

"I'm working, Mom." I dismiss her question.

She tsks, and I clench my teeth together. I'm trying to calm my vibrating body down, ignoring the little voice in my head that wants to argue with her.

"It's a silly job. When will you wake up and come back to work here, son?"

I suck in a deep breath through my nose and breathe out through my mouth, needing to calm the tension that's running through me. The *silly job* is keeping me happy and busy at the moment while I try to figure out the next step in my career.

"I won't take your offer."

"Why? She's perfect and you're not getting any younger."

I close my eyes and bang my head repeatedly on the headrest.

"What's the point of this call? I need to take James's call." Even though he isn't calling, I need to end this conversation now.

"Will you come for dinner on Sunday? Your sister will be here."

I sigh, feeling the tension melt away at the mention of my little sister. "Yeah, I'll be there. I gotta go, but I'm not talking about this tonight. I won't change my mind."

She sighs and mumbles, "Fine. See you at five. Don't be late."

"Yes, Mother." I hang up and throw the phone.

I have met this woman a few times that Mom wants me to marry, and while she seems nice, there's nothing romantic between us. Mom keeps telling me that this woman is happy to marry me, but I can't reciprocate, and it pained me to have to tell her that, but I can't fake a marriage with a woman I felt nothing for. It's not me. I'm not about to pretend or force myself to like her because it's not fair to her either. She deserves someone to love her. And that will never be me. I've seen my friend fall in love, and it might not be something I'm looking for because I'm trying to find myself, but the way he looks at her is full of adoration and love, so if I'm going to get married, it's to someone I feel like that for. If it's meant to be, it will come...and I'll know it.

JONATHAN

"You didn't order those same flowers, did you?" I say into the phone in a hushed voice. I don't want the florist thinking I'm hating on her flowers. James will kick my ass if he can't order his precious flowers for Abigail anymore.

I peer around and browse past the cabinets along the sides of the shop, wondering what's on there. There are new items this week, and I can't help but look while I'm on the phone.

"No, you'll be happy to know I chose something else," he taunts me in an amused voice. I don't know if last week's allergic reaction will ever live a day down.

I grumble into the phone, "I'll have you know I don't trust your choices now."

James chuckles. "If this one isn't good either, how about I make you a deal?"

I stop browsing and lift my head, liking the sound of this. "I'm listening."

"You can choose the next arrangement."

I snort. "That sounds fucking awful."

James's laugh bellows in my ear, and when he recovers, he says, "Well, that's all I got for you. Now shut up and go give my girl her flowers."

"Fine. I'm on it."

As I look up toward the desk, I see *her*. Her dark hair is straight today...and it looks fresh. Like she stepped out of the hairdresser's.

I run my hand through my hair, and my feet are moving, closing the distance and pushing me in her direction. I hang up and stuff the phone inside my pocket. She doesn't notice me approach, because she's too busy taking in the different flowers.

She has dark jeans, a navy top, and sneakers on today. I love this effortless look. She's sexy without even trying, unlike most girls in my parents' circle.

This is my type—a woman who can be casual and herself. I'm sick of women coming on to me for my looks and money. No, I want something real. A real woman. And there's something real about the woman who I'm now standing behind. She turns and looks up with wide eyes before her face softens in recognition.

I can't help but smile like a goofy kid at her. "Hey."

She offers me a smile back and a cute, "Hi."

I glance at the flowers in her hand and frown when I realize they aren't her usual purple saffron flowers, but just simple red roses.

"You're looking at something other than saffron." I point at her bundle.

Her lips part, and my chest warms. The look of surprise does things to me.

"How did you know I get saffron?" Her cheeks and nose have the cutest dusting of pink, and she looks adorable.

"I heard you and the florist talking."

"Oh." She nibbles at her lip, and I wonder if I'm making her nervous.

"You thought I was some crazy stalker?" I tease.

"No. But I won't lie; I was a little freaked out for a second."

"I promise I'm harmless." I hold up my hands in surrender.

She lifts a brow and is biting back a laugh. "I'm supposed to trust your word for it?"

I shrug. "I guess so."

We have both turned completely to face each other.

I tuck my hands into my pockets as she has hers tightly gripped to the bouquet.

"Well, we kind of missed a step that makes trust form." She breaks the silence lingering between us.

"We did?" I ask with a curious expression.

"Mm-hmm."

She extends her hand out, and I look down at it and then back at her face. She sports a grin, and her eyes glimmer with kindness.

"Ruby."

I can't help but smile. She is so freakin' adorable.

I slip my hand in hers and a buzz of electricity hits me. Not only does her hand fit perfectly in mine, but it's so soft and warm I don't want to let go. "John. It's nice to meet you, Ruby."

"It's nice to meet you too."

"Does this mean you can trust me now?"

"Listen, I wouldn't go that far, but it's definitely a start." She returns her hand to the bouquet with a smile.

"Well, that's all I can ask for—"

"Hi, sorry to keep you both waiting." The owner's rushed voice has us both spinning around to face her. "Who can I help first?" she asks, her eyes darting between Ruby and me.

I gesture to Ruby with an outstretched hand and she does the same, which causes our hands to crash. The touch doesn't last because she pulls back and I'm apologizing straight away.

"So sorry. I guess we both had the same idea," I say and see her touch her lips with that same hand, rubbing it mindlessly, and I follow the movement, transfixed.

"It's okay. You go first. I'm not in a rush." She has an unusually high pitch in her voice.

"Ladies first," I encourage.

"I agree. Ruby, I'll serve you first and I'll be back to you." Sally says.

I nod. "Take your time."

Ruby smiles. "Thank you."

"Anytime."

Instead of looking away, I watch her walk to the saffron, surprised when she peers over her shoulder and bites her lip before dipping her head. She turns back to focus on whatever the owner is talking about. I watch her grab the bunch of purple flowers and wander to the counter to pay. When she leaves, she smiles and waves at me as she passes. I'm still frozen to the spot, but I wave, which makes her smile larger.

I don't fucking wave to anyone, but my brain misfires whenever she is around.

"Okay, let me grab your order." I hear the owner say, pulling my eyes away from Ruby.

I walk to the counter. "Thanks. I didn't catch your name," I say, hating that I don't know her name and I've been in here a few times now. It's rude and unlike me. I'm going to blame the dazzling brunette named Ruby. I need to shake off these new emotions that have seemed to take over my brain.

"Sally."

"John."

She picks up a bunch and hands it over. I'm relieved to see the god-awful lilies aren't there. These are a mix of pinks and whites, and as I hold it, nothing seems to cause my eyes or throat to itch...for now. Not wanting to take my chances, I leave.

But as I exit the door, I pause mid-step. Ruby is standing next to the door with a pale face and big round eyes, clutching her flowers so tight she's squishing them. My heart races at her frightened look, and I don't hesitate taking my next step to her.

RUBY

"RUBY?" JOHN'S VOICE CUTS through the still air.

I hesitantly turn to face him. His face is etched with hard lines, and I realize since I left before him, it probably seems strange that I'm standing glued to the shop window. It's currently keeping me feeling safe.

Peeling my back from the window, I stand straight and try to not be as affected as I feel, but I wonder if I'm too late. "Ah. Hi."

My voice sounds strained.

"Are you okay? How come you're still here?" He's standing close and his scent washes over me. I stare back into his brown eyes, losing myself in them as I debate internally.

Do I tell him the truth, or will he think I'm crazy?

When I peer down, I swallow hard at the flowers he's holding. He might be in a hurry to deliver them to...

A special someone?

The green-eyed monster wants to be jealous, but the fear wins. The jealous part of me is too tired to care.

I rub the back of my neck where tension is building. "I'm sorry. I shouldn't be bothering you. You're probably off to meet someone to give them flowers."

His brows draw down in a deep-set frown. "These aren't for me. I'm picking these up for my boss to deliver them to his girlfriend."

I let out a deep breath and feel the flutter of worry leave me at hearing that. Maybe he doesn't have anyone? I try not to get ahead of myself and remember why I'm not at Grandma's house right now. But I'm struggling with my words.

"Okay."

He touches my arm and tenderly strokes it up and down in the most soothing manner as his eyes bore into mine. "Ruby, what's going on?" His tone is stern, and it seems to have me spilling the truth.

"I, um, feel like something is off," I whisper, my gaze scanning the surrounding area at the mention of the eerie feeling.

His brows pinch together, but he doesn't say anything, obviously waiting for me to finish, so I continue.

"It's like someone is behind me...following me. And I had a note left on my car last week saying, *I miss you*."

I swallow hard past the tightness that's forming in my throat.

He straightens and scans the vicinity. "Let me have a look around and then I'm walking you to your car."

Not feeling comfortable walking on my own, I simply nod. I know I'll feel better if he does. "I'm probably overthinking it, but it's never happened before."

"It's better to be safe than sorry. And I want you safe."

Those words wash over me, blanketing me in their warmth. Panic has rendered me speechless, so I don't feel that tingling that I usually might at his words.

He grabs my hand and threads his fingers through mine. Our palms touch, and it feels oddly easy. I should be more freaked out that this guy I barely know is holding my hand, but I can't even think, let alone walk straight, so holding his hand is keeping me from falling over. But I feel I can trust him. With my line of work, my gut is what I follow, so now shouldn't be any different.

He walks in front of me to keep me sheltered behind him. I follow his steps, gripping his hand like a safety net.

He peeks over his shoulder. "Are you okay?"

I nod.

"I can't find anything suspicious. Where's your car?"

I hadn't been paying any attention, but I look up and take my surroundings in and immediately recognize the street where I'd parked my car.

"Just over on the right." I don't want to disconnect our hands, so I nod toward the street where it is.

"This way?"

"Yeah, across the street. The silver one."

I move so I'm beside him. It's strange to walk with a guy, hand in hand, like a couple. I smile, thinking about telling my grandma when I get to her place. She'll drill me with questions about him, and as soon as she gets a hint he is hot, she will want me to go on a date with him, or worse, meet him.

I'm not afraid anymore with him beside me. I just hope whoever it is doesn't return.

What if the person comes back next week? Will he be there?

I can't expect him to save me every time. I have to put my big girl panties on and protect myself. I've never been scared or vulnerable, and I think it's derailing my sense of control. I don't like being pushed into unfamiliar territory.

We cross the road, and as we approach my car, I know it's time to untangle our hands. Even though I don't want to. We stop beside the car and part our hands.

I cradle the saffron as I stare up into his dark gaze. "Thanks for doing this. You didn't have to, but I appreciate it."

"Anytime. I'm glad you were sensible and waited by the shop. It was the safest option. And I'm glad I left after you and you weren't stuck there." An unreadable expression flashes across his face, and I can't imagine what he's thinking, but if it's anything like me...it's what would've happened if he wasn't there? Would I still be there waiting, terrified?

I shrug off the thought because I'm not there anymore. I'm here. Safe. Thanks to him.

I fetch my keys out of my bag and unlock the car door. He moves over and opens the door. I take my seat and carefully lay the flowers on the passenger seat and turn to face him with a smile. "Thanks again."

He leans down, resting his chin on his hands on top of the doorframe. "I'll see you next week?"

I can't help but feel relieved knowing he will be there, but I need to figure out a way to protect myself. He can't be expected to be there every single time. I can't ask that of him either.

"Definitely," I say with a small, shy grin.

"Good. Now, before you go, can I grab your number? I want you to text me when you get to your destination. To make sure you're okay. You trust me now, right?"

The way my heart races for him, I don't hesitate.

"Yes, I trust you."

We exchange numbers before he closes the door with a wink. I bite my lip, hiding a stupidly happy smile. He walks off, and I watch his handsome frame move along the sidewalk before I drive off, already excited to see him next week.

Jonathan

I'm typing away on my work computer at White Empire, but my mind wanders off. I rub my freshly shaved chin as I realize I know nothing about her.

I didn't even get her last name yesterday, and if I text her now, she'll think I'm weird and she's already freaked out.

Grabbing my phone from my pocket, I open her text from yesterday, and I can't help but smile.

Ruby: Home. Safe. Thanks again. :)

Dropping my phone back down on the desk, I refocus on my task at hand, but frustration gets the better of me.

She rattles my brain to not even get her last name.

I keep tapping my finger on the desk, when an idea strikes me. Her social media handles. Surely her last name will come up there. Then I can see if anything is abnormal for someone to be leaving her a note and giving her this unsettled feeling.

Like an ex...

I bring up Facebook and type in Ruby, but it's a popular name, and after spending an hour clicking on every profile listed, I almost give up. None of them matches the woman I'm looking for. She's hard to forget, after all.

Those pouty, kissable lips. That long beautiful hair...I want to run my hands through as I kiss her.

Yeah, I know I would have seen her.

Her beauty would have stood out on the screen in front of me.

Disappointed, I sigh.

Dead end after dead fucking end.

Her full name is important for me, so I can eliminate whoever's making her feel unsafe. Terrorized.

I don't see her as crazy. I believe her.

I don't want to see that scared, paled face ever again. She should walk the streets comfortably.

Definitely not her. I don't want her scared. I'll do anything I can to protect her.

After finishing my typing, I sip my coffee, still holding on to the hope I'll find an answer. My phone rings, and when I see who it is, I sigh. *James*.

"I need you to take me over to Browns," he says after I answer.

"Right now?"

"Yes. Now."

"I'm coming," I say and shut down my computer. It's not like I have anything to go off, so this is a welcomed distraction.

But as I'm about to hang up, James asks, "What's up?"

Not wanting to discuss it right now, I say, "I'll tell you when I see you."

"Okay. See you soon." He hangs up, and I stuff my phone in my pocket and go downstairs.

A couple of minutes later, I'm waiting in the car when James opens the door and slides across the backseat, typing away on his phone, so I wait until he finishes and puts his seatbelt on and looks up at me before I drive away.

"What's going on?" he asks with a puzzled expression.

"Every Friday, whenever I go to the florist to pick up your arrangement for Abby, there has been this woman."

James's eyebrow lifts at the word *woman.*

"Interesting," James murmurs.

I push his words aside and continue with the story. I'm hoping verbalizing it will bring some new ideas.

"So yesterday, she left before me, but when I left the shop, she was standing by the door, frightened. She said someone had left an, *I miss you* note on her car and she felt something was off. Like someone was following her."

James's eyes don't waver as he waits for me to finish before he speaks.

"I looked around, but nothing or no one seemed out of place." I breathe out the frustration I feel.

"She's not some freak, is she?"

I clench my hands on the steering wheel as I drive, causing my knuckles to turn white. "No."

Why the fuck would he think that?

"And you say you've only met her twice?" James questions further.

"Yeah," I say, confused by his comment.

"You seem invested in her." He rubs his hand over his jaw.

My chest warms as I think of her, knowing there is something about her that has me under her thumb. But when he asks, my defensive mode turns on.

"So, anyway, as I was saying. I was trying to figure out what to do about this guy or girl who might have been following her. I looked around and then eventually walked her to her car and told her to text me when she got home."

James's brows lift. "You got her number?"

"Yeah, I wanted to make sure she was fine."

"That's all? You're not interested in her?"

I think for a second—do I answer this honestly or lie? He's my buddy. If I can't trust him, then I can't trust anyone.

"Well, yes, I'm interested in her. But why, I don't know. I just...there's something about her, James."

When silence lingers for a few minutes, I glance at him through the rearview mirror and witness his smirk. He's enjoying every second of this.

"I did some research, but because I only know her first name, I'm unable to look her up."

His smirk drops and he sits up. "Do you need any help from me? You know I have connections."

"I would normally say no, but, James, I think...yes."

He pulls out his phone and quickly types away on it before his eyes meet mine.

"I need to ask her first," I say when I realize we might be breaching her privacy.

"You want to ask her?" he asks, confused.

"Yes. I feel like it's an invasion of privacy to look into her, her friends, exes and family. All behind her back. I know I wouldn't like it if it was done to me."

He shakes his head. "If you say so."

"I say so, James. I just...she seems the type that would want to be asked." I pause before continuing. "I see her saying yes. But just to be sure, I want to ask. If she tells me to back off, I'll respect her wishes. So yes, I would love to meet your connection and have a chat with them and try to figure out what's going on. I don't like a woman frightened and scared on the street."

"Yeah, totally, no woman should feel like that. I'll send you the details in a text now." He returns to his phone, and a second later, my phone chimes with a new text.

I park on the side of the road. "Well, we're here now, James."

His head lifts to peer out the window before unbuckling.

"Thanks for the number," I say.

"No worries. I'll see you soon." James exits the car, and when he closes the door, I take a deep breath.

I'm at the florist's shop the following Friday with the stupidest smile on my face. I get to see *her*. But the further I walk and linger waiting for Sally to serve me, I realize Ruby's not here yet.

I'm a little sad. I enjoyed seeing her every week. It was something I looked forward to.

I miss the electricity sizzling between us, our easy chat, the warmth at holding each other's hand. The charge is unlike anything I've experienced, and when she's around, it's there. Even in a scary moment. I knew she felt calm with me. Her breathing wasn't quick; she didn't seem distressed. With her labored breaths, I can only hope it was me who calmed her. And I have to admit, it made me feel good. I like the fact that she can rely on me. I just hope I can figure out what this weird sense she got is before it's too late.

I swallow hard, hating that thought. No fucking way will I let anything happen to her.

"Hi, John," Sally says, and I turn to face her, grateful she's taking me away from my thoughts.

"Hi, Sally. I'm here to pick up James's arrangement."

"Yes, right. I'll grab it. Come, follow me."

As I walk behind her, I can't bite my tongue any longer. "Um, so, Ruby...is she coming in today?"

"Ruby?" Sally asks with a knowing smile before continuing to speak. "Well, she normally does, but she's a little late today. All right, now give me a second, and I'll be straight back with the arrangement."

"Where does she go on Fridays?" I say a little louder because Sally is walking further away than usual to pick up this week's arrangement. But as she walks toward me, I see these flowers are taller.

What the fuck has he ordered now?

"She goes to her grandma's house with the saffron and cooks using them every Friday." Sally smiles at me when she lowers the flowers to the desk.

The knowledge of Ruby warms my heart. A woman who treats her family like that is a woman worth keeping. She's wholesome, beautiful, and everything I could want.

I need to marry someone like her.

I don't know care if she doesn't have what my parents are after—money and/or a family name.

My stomach rolls at all the thoughts. Why can't love be enough for them? A connection so powerful it makes my heart beat its own rhythm for her.

I grab the flowers with difficulty because of their size. I'm going to tell James these are way too obnoxious; Abigail won't like these. I know I fucking don't.

I plaster on a fake smile. "Thanks, Sally. I'll see you next week."

"See you, John."

I walk slowly from the shop, hoping I might catch Ruby on my way. But as I step outside and look around, that flicker of hope diminishes.

Maybe next week?

RUBY

As I'm almost at Sally's door, a hand touches my shoulder. I turn around swiftly and press down on the can of pepper spray I bought myself.

"Ah, fuck," he screams.

Shit! No, that's John.

Horrified, I watch as John bends over and furiously rubs his eyes, still cursing. I'm frozen on the spot, unable to move to help him.

"What the fuck?" he says.

"Oh my god, I'm so sorry," I say, shoving the can back into my handbag. And then cover my open mouth. I peer around and there are now passersby staring as they wander past and it makes me more embarrassed.

I've been on edge lately, so his touch on my shoulder scared the crap out of me and caused me to react without thinking.

"It fucking burns." He's still muttering under his breath. My stomach churns at the pain I've caused.

"I'm so sorry, John. I just...I thought...I don't know what I was thinking. Just not that it would be you."

He tries to stand and open his eyes, but he can't, so he stays hunched over. "It's okay. It's not your fault. You did good by buying it, but this fucking sucks."

His words are nicer than I deserve, and I know he's trying to make me feel better, but my heart is still racing and I'm struggling to swallow the lump in my throat. I don't even know what to do to fix his pain.

I want to touch him, but I don't want to make things worse. So, I just stand awkwardly, hoping a passerby can help us.

"It's easing," he says as he straightens.

I'm still staring at him like a deer in headlights. "I'm so sorry again. Can I grab something? Let's get inside and see if Sally can help."

"Good idea." He nods.

Without thinking, I grab onto his upper arm so that I can be his vision. "Let's get you inside. Just keep your eyes closed."

I push open the door and drag him along, appreciating the feeling of his tricep flexing underneath my hand. He's so strong and sexy.

I can't deny that a little flutter happens in my stomach and between my thighs at his muscles. I haven't touched a man in ages.

He's all man, that's for sure. I drag him along through the shop and scan around to find Sally. She spots us approaching her, and her brows pinch together in concern. "What's going on?" she asks.

John groans beside me, and it's like I'm doused by a bucket of cold water. Gone are the flutters and aches and now it's replaced with guilt.

"Well, I kind of pepper sprayed him," I say in a low voice before biting my lips.

Sally's face lightens with humor, and she chuckles.

He groans in pain, and it causes me to become protective of us.

"It's not funny, Sally. It was an accident. I've just not been feeling myself. So I carried one and he touched me and I sprayed him. I need your help. I don't know what to do, but I need to ease his pain. I don't know what else to do. I never looked up what to do when you spray someone." I want to explain myself but also get her to understand my concern. Like what if I've caused him permanent damage?

"Okay, okay, let's go over to my computer and have a look." Sally says.

Great, we're about to use Dr. Google. I want a real doctor or nurse, but there's no one around. I take a breath and guide him along and follow Sally to her computer. She types something in.

We follow the flushing instructions she found online, and he's able to open his eyes and look at me. His beautiful brown eyes are red rimmed, and I suddenly feel sick, hating how I've let my mind wander off and think someone is following me.

Seriously, why am I doing this to myself? Buying pepper spray was a stupid idea.

You brought it to protect yourself.

"John, I'm sorry. Your eyes are red," I say as I stare at him.

He reaches out to grab my arm, but then drops it back to his side. I'm sure he's too scared to touch me, but I want him to touch me. I don't want him to hold back. Fuck, this is a disaster.

"It's okay. I want you to protect yourself. This is not a bad thing. At least you tried. It sucks at the time." He tries to laugh to make me feel better, but it doesn't help. My stomach is still rolling in waves of guilt and embarrassment.

I offer a half smile. "I bet. It's never been sprayed in my eyes before."

His face brightens, and my nose scrunches as I try to figure out what he's beaming at.

"Well, I think I owe you a drink now. Or should I say, you owe me a coffee date now." A wicked smile forms on his face, and now, I know why his expression changed so quickly. I can't help but smile back; he's piqued my interest and offered me a date. I can't exactly say no, can I?

Sally smirks at our interaction. And I'm sure she's loving every second of this.

"As in…now," he says.

I was not expecting him to want to go right this second. As if reading my face that's etched in surprise, he says, "If you're free. Or would you like to meet up another time?"

Knowing I'm only going to my grandma's and she would have a field day knowing I had a real date with a guy, I wonder, *Why not?* I'm going to have to tell her about this story anyway. So, I may as well have something else to follow up with while we bake our pie.

"All right, let's go today."

He beams. "Perfect."

Sally can't contain her grin at our exchange, it seems. Not indulging her, I ask, "Can I pick my bouquet up afterward?"

Her eyes twinkle in delight as she answers smugly, "Of course. You two have a good time. I'll get them ready."

"Thanks, Sally," John adds with a smile.

I dip my chin and walk out of the shop with a heated face, and I can't deny the tingle that runs through me by that knowledge. A hot guy wanting to go on a date with...me? *Sign me up.*

He stays close behind me as if once again protecting me. The way he acts...it's as if he doesn't want me to be too far out of his range.

I like this feeling of being around him. He gives me the sense of security and safety I crave. Especially while I don't even know if someone's watching me. Or maybe I'm reading into nothing. Either way, I'm excited.

It'll be my first real date in over twelve months.

Even if it's only for coffee.

RUBY

"WHERE DID YOU WANT to go?" he asks beside me.

I slow my steps on the sidewalk. His hand brushes mine, and it causes my fingers to twitch. How easy would it be to take his hand in mine at this moment? But I focus back on his question and not on his hand.

I look around at the row of stores, from clothes to pharmacy. "I haven't been to any shops around here before. Do you have any suggestions?"

He shakes his head. "No, I haven't been to any, but I'm sure they're all good. How bad can they screw up coffee?"

My brows raise in disbelief; he's never had a bad coffee before? "I've had bad ones in my time. They burn the beans." The thought makes me screw up my face.

"That's shit. How about that one there?" I follow where he's pointing and nod my head.

"Sounds good."

I continue walking, expecting silence, so I'm surprised when he asks, "How are you feeling after the other night?"

I snort. "Well, I sprayed you with pepper spray. I wouldn't say I'm recovered."

His chest rumbles with a deep chuckle, and it's the sexiest sound. Can this guy for once do something ugly?

But I don't think there's anything ugly about him.

"I'm still on edge. Still worried there is something, or, should I say, *someone* watching me, but another part of me thinks I'm fucking crazy." I laugh, but it's strained. I'm trying not to show how terrified I am of the impending threat.

He reaches out and touches my shoulder and softly strokes my arm, and it leaves a trail of heat. "You're not crazy. Trust your gut. If it's telling you that something's off, it's probably because you're right."

I appreciate his kind words, and it makes me feel a little better. And when he removes his hand from my arm, I almost groan, missing the contact already.

"Mm. Yeah, I guess so. I guess I'll have to trust your word that I'm not crazy, but I'm not sold," I say teasingly, my mouth twisted with an easy smile.

We arrive at the busy café. The sun is shining bright today, so the outside dining area is filled with people. We find a free table nestled in the corner and take a seat. The waitress comes to take our order. I peer over at John. He smiles at me letting me go first.

"Just a cappuccino for me, please," I say.

Maybe I should have ordered a decaf. The caffeine is probably not going to help me rein in my racing pulse.

My gaze moves to him.

"A long black, thanks," he says.

"Any sugar or cream in either of them?" she asks.

We both decline.

When she's out of earshot, we sit there with wide grins on our face.

Now I get to ask him whatever I want. I rub my hands together and think for a moment. When something pops in my mind, I lean on the table with my elbows to focus on him and ask, "What do you do for work that makes you have a Friday off?"

His mouth twitches, and he leans in closer. "I'm a driver."

A driver? Really? He doesn't seem like a driver.

But what do I know?

I really wasn't expecting it, but now I have lots of questions. "Who do you drive for? Do I know them? Are they famous or something?"

He laughs, tipping his head back, showing me his sexy throat, and I can't help but notice a mole on the side of his neck near his right ear. Is it a birthmark?

"No. He's not famous. But he's still cool. He's actually a friend." His words cut through my inspection, and I drag my gaze back to his. He's staring at me with a curious expression.

I look down and suck in a breath before looking up to speak. "Oh, yeah?" I eagerly say, wanting him to tell me more.

He reclines back and runs his hand through his hair before dropping it into his lap.

"We grew up together. His name is James White. He's a real estate property developer. And he owns a building called White Estate."

"Wow, that's impressive."

He nods. "Yeah, he's a good guy. And it's easy. I can't complain."

"Well, that's good, I guess. Is that...all you do?" I try to say it kindly, but it's hard to imagine him only driving a CEO around.

"No," he says, but I don't miss the flicker of an expression I can't decipher.

Like a painful one.

He runs his hand through his hair before leaning on the table to speak. "Well, I used to be in IT. Like a family business thing. But I needed to get out."

Seeing the look on his face tells me I don't want to push because it seems like a difficult topic for him. He's opened up enough already.

He changes the subject by asking, "And what do you do that lets *you* have every Friday off?"

He wiggles his brows at me, wearing a cheeky smirk.

"I'm a social worker," I say proudly, knowing how much I love my job.

"Wow." His jaw slackens. "It's not surprising, though."

I frown. "What do you mean?"

"You're kind, warm, and easy to talk to. I feel like it's a fitting job for you."

I smile at his words, but the blush rising on my cheeks has me averting my gaze for a moment to get myself in check. I've never been affected by a guy before, so this is all new. To have him genuinely talking about me in a positive, sweet way is unusual, but very nice. He makes all my previous boyfriends look pathetic. They thought my job was ridiculous and encouraged me to study something else. So having him compliment it warms my heart.

I lock gazes with him. "Thank you. I work Monday to Thursday and Saturday."

"Is there any particular reason for that?"

The waitress interrupts us by dropping our coffees off.

I take a sip before going back to our conversation. "Well, I'm close with my parents and my grandma, but my grandma's elderly now. So, I spend every Friday baking." I laugh and continue, "It's why I buy the saffron."

"What do you make with the saffron?" he asks as he sips his coffee.

"Pies." I chew the inside of my cheek. The way he's staring is making my heart pound. There is so much warmth in his eyes.

"Well, that's cool," he says, lowering his drink.

"I think so. And it's not like a savory pie, it's a sweet pie."

There's this flicker of a funny expression on his face that makes me see where his mind's gone.

Boys.

I giggle and take a sip of my coffee, thinking how easy it is, sitting here with him, chatting.

I know I do it for a living, but that's work. This is just...he's easy. Easy to be around. Easy to fall for and obviously easy on the eyes.

Men are normally way more complicated than this. He just makes it comfortable right away. What's the catch?

He sips his coffee, and I assess him over my cup with curiosity.

When I recall his order, I ask him, "How do you drink that with no cream? It's...awful."

He chuckles. "Yeah, it's not great at the start, but I quickly got used to the taste."

I tip my head back, confused. "So why don't you add some cream or sugar, then?"

"Lower calories," he answers with a shrug.

I'm shocked at that answer, not expecting him to worry about calories, but I remember the feel of his strong tricep underneath my hand, so him watching his calories makes sense. *I can't even imagine what's underneath his clothes.*

I clear my throat, feeling a little flustered from my thoughts. "Well, I like calories. A lot. I don't care what I look like."

He's staring at me intensely, and I sink in the chair a little under his heated gaze.

He leans forward, running his eyes over my body. "You don't need to. You look damn perfect."

"Oh." It comes out as a squeak. I bring the coffee to my lips, needing to wet my parched throat.

I'm still startled when I lower the cup back down to the plate. I don't know what to do. I'm staring at him back...lost. What do you say to a hot guy who's complimenting you about your body and how good you look? It's not something I'm used to.

It's always expected for a woman to count calories and exercise. I've done that in the past and it's exhausting. I just couldn't do it anymore. Losing weight and toning up used to be on my New Year's resolutions every year until I got sick of getting into the second month and feeling like a failure. So, I stopped worrying and I feel better than ever.

I look down at my drink to avoid his gaze because it's causing a heat to form between my thighs.

"So...the flowers are for?" I blurt, finally thinking of something that won't encourage my body to combust.

"James, my boss. He buys his girlfriend flowers every week."

"Oh." I swoon, and add with a wide grin, "How sweet is that?"

"I don't know about sweet. Finding myself in a florist's shop every week wasn't part of my job description. And now it seems I'm stuck doing it," he grumbles with a shake of his head. "You should have seen his order the other week. It was the most ridiculous order of flowers. I was so itchy and my throat and eyes were so sore, I thought my face was gonna blow out."

I giggle at him. He still seems so angry about it.

"I was having some friggin' reaction. I told him if he was ever to buy them again, he can pick up his own flowers or I'm paying for delivery."

I giggle more. "Why doesn't he pay for delivery?" I ask.

He rolls his eyes and air quotes to mock James. "He wants the *personal touch*."

I bring my hands to my chest. "Oh my god, this guy is so sweet. I need to meet him."

"He's taken, remember?" he says in a clipped tone.

Is that jealousy?

I wave my hands and try to explain. "Oh no, it's just, you know, guys like him are scarce. No men think of personal touches. It's rare."

He simply watches me, absorbing the words as I say them. His face is tight before he shivers and blurts out, "Oh, and last week, he ordered these obnoxious, tall ones. It was just ridiculous. Again, I told him if he ordered them again, I will not do his dirty work. He can deliver his own flowers. Speaking of last week, where were you?"

My heart swells, thinking he missed me...did he? Maybe I should play on this and lighten up the mood.

"Are you sure you're not my stalker?" I narrow my eyes, trying to be serious for a second but failing and laughing at my own joke, and when he joins me, I laugh harder.

"No chance," he says.

After we calm down from our fit, we sit there with stupid smiles on our face, looking at each other for a moment while we finish our drinks.

The waitress comes over and we squabble about who pays. He actually looks mortified by my suggesting it. I give up and say if that makes him happy, he can pay. So, he does.

When we leave, he walks me to Sally's. Again, we're back in a comfortable silence. And my mind drifts to wanting to hold his hand, but I can't. We don't have an excuse now like we did before, and I'm not making the first move.

After picking up our orders at Sally's, he walks me to my car and says, "Goodbye. I'll see you next week." As I sit down, he holds the door, pausing, and speaks again. "Oh, can I ask you a question?"

I lift my brow, wondering what he needs to ask me. "Yeah, what's up?"

"James gave me an investigator's number. But I will not use it unless you allow me to. It's your choice, but I would like to see if there's anything strange going on and try to figure out who this person is."

I blink rapidly in shock. Oh, this man. The fact he's thinking of me and willing to find an investigator—this is all so unexpected, but also sweet.

"Well, I can't see why not. And James sounds like a nice guy. So, I trust you and James to have a good investigator, and I can't keep living my life in fear and holding around pepper spray and spraying people I like." I tug my lip between my teeth as the last two words leave my lips.

I watch the moment it dawns on him. His expression darkens with fire, as the electricity bounces between us.

"You like me?" he says, and I can hear the smile in his voice.

I blush. "Yes."

"I like you too," he says, and I turn crimson.

I'm lost in the euphoria of him feeling the same about me. I miss half of what he says and only pick up the next piece.

"I need your last name. And I'll give it to the investigator today."

I nod and give him my last name without hesitation. Knowing it's getting looked into properly has the heaviness lift away from my shoulders. I just hope they discover who, and more importantly, why they are doing this.

"How about next Friday? Before we pick up our flowers, we meet here again?" he asks with a wicked grin.

I blink, shocked at what I'm hearing. He's asking me out again?

I already can't wait for the next week.

Ruby

I'm stirring the cake mixture in the bowl at Grandma's. She stands beside me, watching intently to make sure I'm doing it right. No matter how many times I bake with her, she always hovers and corrects me.

"What's new, sweetheart?"

Here goes nothing.

A smile erupts on my face as I think about John. "Well, I've had a strange couple of weeks."

"A couple of weeks, and I'm only hearing about this now?" Grandma asks.

"Well, I kind of had an incident today, and it's funny, but kind of not."

"What do you mean?" She grabs a spoon to stir the already mixed batter. So, I lean my hip against the counter and fold my arms.

"Well, I've been going to the florist for a while now to pick up our saffron. And last month, I met this—"

She cuts me off. "Gentleman."

I roll my eyes at her excitement. "Calm down. You could be wrong."

"But I'm not, am I?" She gives me a dazzling grin, and I can't help but laugh.

I shake my head. "No, you never are."

She pauses mixing to face me and talk. "Sorry, but you never talk about a man. And the way your face is lighting up right now, I can tell he's special. I need to know every single detail, Ruby."

He is special, but I'm trying not to get ahead of myself.

"Okay, well, so we've been seeing each other on Fridays. He's a driver for his friend but also a successful IT guy. I actually don't know all the details yet, but he picks up flowers for his boss and drops them off every Friday. So, I'd been seeing him at Sally's, but the other week I was leaving to come here, and I just felt off." I cross my arms at the memory.

"What do you mean, sweetheart? What felt off? Were you sick?" She frowns before returning to mixing.

"No, nothing like that. How do I explain this? The air around me didn't feel right. It was as if someone was watching me. After the note, I thought I was crazy. I kind of still think I'm just being paranoid for no reason."

She goes to pour the mixture into the cake pan, so to help, I hold it for her. "Maybe, honey, but that's serious."

I sigh. "I know, I know. Anyway, I'll get to the end of the story and then you can tell me what you think. Because I need your advice." Grandma turns to take the tin to the oven.

"So, he walks me to the car after checking around. We found nothing that didn't look out of order or anyone lurking. And then I came here and forgot about it. In the meantime, I bought myself some pepper spray."

Grandma prepares the tea kettle. "Good idea. Protect yourself."

"Exactly, and today, before I walked into Sally's, he touched my shoulder, and I grabbed my pepper spray and sprayed him."

Grandma laughs hysterically. "You pepper sprayed the lovely man? Oh my. What did you do that for?"

I place my hands on my hips. "In my defense, I didn't see him. He snuck up on me and grabbed my shoulder."

She shakes her head, still chuckling. "Well, that's true. That's his fault."

"But I still felt awful. You should have seen him, crouched over in pain. And when he could open his eyes, they were so red and raw. And then he told me I had to go to coffee with him to make up for it."

Grandma grabs the cups so I grab the tea bags and put them in the cups.

She smiles. "Ohhh, so he asked you on a date?"

"No. Calm down." I giggle, walking to get the creamer from the fridge.

"It sounds like it was a date." She murmurs, as I pour the creamer in both the cups.

"I barely know him," I argue. It's more to myself than to her. I'm reminding myself I need to take it slow.

Cradling the cup, I take a sip, enjoying the warm, milky drink.

"So what? Growing up, I met your grandfather, and after a week, my family married us off. That was how it was done."

Meeting her gaze, I explain, "It's different now. You get to marry who you want, who you love, and who you want to spend your time with."

"I get that, but what I'm saying is that you don't need to worry about how long you've known each other before you get together or marry."

"No marriage! That's not going to happen. Now there's something else he mentioned that I want to discuss with you, though."

"Yeah?" she says as she takes her cup over to the table to sit down, and I follow her, taking my tea to join her.

"We went to get coffee, and he told me about James, his boss. He had given him a contact for an investigator.

He could arrange it if I want this matter to be investigated further."

"That's kind of them. I hope you said yes, dear."

I nod. "I think that it's a good idea because I just hate this weird feeling I'm getting, and the fact I pepper sprayed him, it's just so embarrassing. Like I can't be spraying everyone and staying freaked out all my life."

"Well, that's fair enough. I hope they find this person responsible. I can't have something happening to my favorite granddaughter."

I sip my tea and answer with a smile, "You mean your only one."

"Exactly."

"Anyway, I'll see what he comes back with. He said we should meet at the same coffee shop before we pick up our flowers next week."

She smiles, and her eyes are sparkling with excitement. "Another date. This is exciting."

"Calm down. I'm not about to marry him."

"I didn't say that, dear." She smirks as she sips her tea, the smell of the cake filling the house.

I sit watching her, knowing she's already picturing a wedding in her head.

"Well, if you don't get married, let's hope you get laid."

My mouth drops open, horrified. "What?"

"Maybe that would help you with stress. There's nothing wrong with being hot and heavy with a handsome guy. And you wouldn't be like this if he was not tall, dark, and handsome. That's your type, right?"

I know she remembers what my ex looks like, and I can't deny I have a type.

"Yes, but—"

She cuts me off. "But nothing, sweetheart. You need to go and live. You're young, fit, and healthy, so go and bang him senseless."

She never stops amazing me. I am mortified, and when I find my voice, I say, "I'm just meeting him so he can tell me what the investigator finds. That's it! There will be no banging or getting laid or whatever other word you want to use about it. There is none of that going down. Thank you very much."

Oh god, this conversation is awkward. I rub my forehead and try to slow my breathing down.

"Why, honey? Sex is good, it's healthy."

Oh my god, please stop.

I squeeze my eyes shut before looking at her. "Yeah, well, not a conversation I want to have with my grandma, but you are unique."

"And I'm fine with that. You need that little bit of a push in life. You always work so hard, and you never have any pleasure."

"Oh my god," I say, wincing. "Get your mind out of the gutter. There will be no sex involved."

It's as if I'm saying it to myself as much as I'm saying it to her.

"What's his name?" she asks, and I smile.

"John."

"Nice. An old-fashioned name. I'm loving this guy already. Maybe you could bring him over here?" Her face is hopeful, but I need to cut that off quickly.

"No way. You'll bring up marriage or sex. I think I'll die of embarrassment. I've already done a big enough job by spraying him with the pepper spray."

"No. I'll be on my best behavior." She shakes her head softly before sipping more of her tea.

"It's not happening. I don't want to give him the wrong impression."

Her expression softens. "And you don't want more?"

If he asked me, I'd say yes, but that's not going to happen.

"Well, I just don't know. My head is just...I need to figure out what's going on with this weird stalking issue. And I also want to spend more time with him and talk to him and get to know him. I'm not about to jump into bed or into a relationship with someone I barely know."

"Okay, I understand that, but I hope you don't keep him in the friend zone. If you do like him, you need to tell him."

"If the opportunity arises, and he asks, then I'll answer him honestly."

The timer for the oven goes off, and I pull out the cake from the oven. It allows me time to think about her words.

I do like him.

I wonder if he likes me...

Jonathan

It's Friday and I get to see her again. Every time I think of her, I have excitement pulsing through me.

I'm meeting her at the cafe, so I get there a bit earlier than planned, to make sure that she's safe and that nothing happens to her on her way to meet me. Unfortunately, the investigator has found nothing yet. Everything's coming up empty, but he's promised me he'll keep working around the clock on it, and that he won't give up.

I peer at my watch. She should be here any minute. The cafe is busy again and there's lots of chatter around me. I sit outside where we did last time, excited to be spending more time with her.

After a couple of minutes, I see her get out of her car. And I can't help but watch as she takes every step as if she's on a catwalk for me. She's in black pants that show off her delicious curves and a blue blouse that enhances her tiny waist. She's so beautiful, and I get to spend the morning having a coffee with her. I couldn't think of anything better.

I have a stupid smile on my face as I watch her walk closer and closer to me.

When she finally notices me, I offer a small wave.

I can't help but be myself with her. Following my heart and not worrying about how it might seem to anyone else.

She smiles at me and gives me a wave back. I could be wrong, but I think she walks a little bit quicker. When she approaches the table, I stand.

"Hey," she says breathlessly.

"Hi. You look beautiful."

Her teeth sink into her pillowy bottom lip and tug it into her mouth, and I feel a rush of heat to my groin. Yeah, she does things to not only mess my head up but my heart and cock too.

"Thanks."

"Come sit. I haven't ordered anything yet."

"Okay." She sits, and I take my seat after her. I want to rip the Band-Aid off and tell her the bad news first before I spend the rest of the morning getting to know her.

"Well, the investigator hasn't found anything yet. But he's promised to keep looking for me because I'm not happy with that answer."

She puts her hands under her chin and stares at me. "Maybe I am crazy, then." She laughs at herself, but I know it's masking her embarrassment, and I don't want her to feel like that for speaking up when she feels scared.

"No, I think you have a reason to. Let's just wait and see once he's done a full report. At least for now, you have nothing to fear. Have you been jumpy and anxious still? No pepper spraying anybody?"

That gets a real laugh out of her and it's infectious, causing me to laugh with her.

"No, I haven't pepper sprayed anyone else. I'm too scared to even use it after hurting you."

I frown. "Definitely use it if you must. I don't want you ever to feel bad for doing that. You're better off protecting yourself. And it's always better to be safe than sorry."

She nods but stays silent, and the waitress appears. We order our coffees, and she walks away.

"A busy day with Grandma again?"

"Yeah. Our usual of baking pies and having fun. And then getting drilled about who I'm dating and going to marry."

"Oh." My brows rise in surprise.

"Yeah. She wants me married and settled down. And she loves to ask me every week."

I chuckle. "She sounds fun."

She snorts. "Fun to you, maybe. But for me, not so much."

"Fair enough," I say, and I'm about to ask her another question. But from the corner of my eye, I see my mother walking up to the table, dressed in a designer blazer, heels, bag; even her hair and make-up are all fucking done up. She screams of money.

Oh no.

I want to hide, but she's already noticed me. I put on a fake smile, and when she approaches the table, I say, "Hi, Mom."

"Hello, Jonathan."

Fuck, she called me by my real name.

I hate getting called Jonathan. I much prefer being called John. No one else calls me Jonathan other than her and Dad.

"What are you doing here?" she asks, flicking her gaze to Ruby and me, annoyance etched into her face.

"I'm about to go pick up some flowers from across the road for James and Abigail. I've got to drop them off to Abigail from James."

"That's sweet of James, isn't it?" she drawls.

"Yes, it is."

We all know how much she loves James. She loves how rich he is and how he's getting married. She didn't like

Abigail being from a small town, but she seems to have moved on from that, considering how successful James is. It overrides that in her mind.

Ruby clears her throat.

Shit. I have to introduce Ruby to Mom.

"Why don't you introduce me to your friend?"

The way she says "friend" annoys me. I want her to go away.

Instead, I continue, "Mom, this is my friend, Ruby. Ruby, this is my mother."

I don't even bother with names because I don't want her to know my full name, but my mom knows how to ruin my life.

"Monica Black."

I peer over to Ruby to see if that name rings any bells.

It doesn't look like it.

I let out a long breath I was holding. Now, if she hasn't registered Monica Black, then maybe she won't put together my name—Jonathan Black.

It's a name that most people around Chicago know.

"Did you want to sit down, Monica? And join us for coffee," Ruby offers politely, too nice if you ask me. She doesn't realize I'm fighting with them over my future.

I bite my lip to hold back a smile at the way my mother's eye ticks from not getting called Mrs. Black.

"Thanks for the offer, love, and well, I would have joined, but I must get going. I have to meet a friend here."

I sit back in the chair a little to look up at her and ask, "I was wondering what you were doing in this part of town."

"It's not a bad part of town, son. I don't know what you're talking about. It's not my favorite, but you know it has..." She looks around the street before continuing, "It has character."

Meaning it's not classy, in my mom's words.

"I must go now. Ruby, it was lovely to meet you. Maybe I'll catch you again sometime." My mom offers her a fake smile.

Ruby, being the sweet, sincere person she is, offers her a friendly smile and says, "Maybe."

"Bye, Mom," I say.

I bet Mom's gonna drill me about this soon. I'll get the call by four o'clock from her, wanting to know everything about Ruby. So she can investigate her. I know her tricks now.

Once she spins around on her Louis Vuitton and her back is away from us, I feel the air leave my lungs in a sigh. I can breathe easier. The waitress brings our coffee over and I've never looked forward to a drink in my life. But I wish it was a little bit stronger than coffee. I take a sip anyway, relieved at the liquid coating my dry throat.

"Your mother seems nice."

I burst out laughing. "You think that woman is nice? I don't. She's judgmental and stuck up." And I want to say so unlike me, but I think I've been harsh enough.

"She seems nice." She shrugs.

I say nothing back, not wanting to bring this date down. Instead, I sip the coffee and ask her, "How was work this week?"

"It's been pretty good. The usual clients coming in and a few new ones but nothing else. You?"

"Just running around for James as he wins more jobs."

She sips her coffee before lowering it. "What are your plans this weekend?"

"Why? Are you asking me out?" I wiggle my eyebrows in a tease.

We both laugh.

"No, getting to know you." She rolls her eyes in a playful way.

"I know. I'm just teasing you. I'm catching up with friends. You?" I ask, wanting to know how she spends every moment of her weekend without work to entertain her.

"Well, I work Saturday, but otherwise, house chores, and that's about as exciting as it gets."

I wonder what it would be like if she came to my house and we could watch a movie together. It's normally something I do alone, and it would be nice to share it with someone.

We talk for a little bit longer. Both of us now finished our coffees. "Are you ready?" she asks, and I nod.

I get up and pay again, and she doesn't protest this time. Which I'm grateful for. I will always pay for the date.

That's what I'm calling today. Even if she doesn't agree.

I assume she would want this to be a date, but I don't want to push her when she's already stressed over the weirdness she's experiencing.

And now she's discovering the investigator found nothing. I'm sure that's hard to take.

We walk back into the florist's shop together, and I pick up James's order and she picks up her saffron.

"I'll try to give you an update next week."

"Sure. That sounds good," she says with a smile, and it takes my breath away.

"I was hoping you would say that."

RUBY

I'm driving to Grandma's, and I can't stop thinking about his name. And now I know his full name is Jonathan Black. I would never have guessed; I assumed it was 'John.'

Why do I know that name, though?

The other thing swirling around my mind is the way his mom was dressed. She was sophisticated, and she looked expensive. I'm not broke, but I don't have that money. She looked to be on another level. And the way he said, "What are you doing in this part of town," it was like she would never be caught dead here.

He wasn't rude, but he wasn't nice. I get the sense they don't have the best relationship. It's just something in my gut that's telling me something is off between them. But who doesn't have family drama?

Before I get out of my car and into my grandma's house, I quickly pull up my phone and type in his name.

I gasp loudly as the results pop up, one after the other. My hand covers my mouth in shock as I read his stats.

Jonathan Black.

Thirty-five.

Inventor of Integration Software.

Billionaire.

I swear my eyes are seeing things. But how and why is he a driver if he's a billionaire? I just don't get it. I read through a couple more articles, trying to find the answers.

But I can't see where and why. Until I stumble upon one that says there was a squabble between him and his parents. And that he left the family business and his startup business.

I scrunch up my face and try to understand the reason. Why would he leave his business to become his friend's driver?

Who would want to do that?

He never looked like he was a billionaire. But what do they look like anyway? They are normal people too. I shake away that silly thought; it doesn't change him. His status doesn't affect my feelings for him.

He never treated me differently. If I'm honest, I wished he had filled me in on his life. Because his life is in the news and splashed across socials, and if I'm with him, I could also be photographed. Maybe the paparazzi are the ones following me?

But wouldn't we have caught them the other week when we went looking?

I'm blown away, and my head is thumping with a headache forming. I just wish I knew this information before...but what would I've done with it?

The fact I would've known he's invented some-thing—which is damn intelligent—and a billionaire, shouldn't change a thing. He's sweet, caring, sexy, and smart. Taking time out to investigate the weird note and feeling I had. It can't be paparazzi trying to get a photo of me to discover who I am because I received the note before I met him.

But stumbling upon all this information is a shock. I'm gonna have to ask him more questions and let him know what I think.

Ruby: Is it true that you're *the* Jonathan Black? And you left your family business and started your own company?

I delete the message, finding that too rude to send over a text. I plan to speak to him next week at the coffee shop.

This means it will be a helluva long week.

Ruby

I STARE OVER MY cup at him. I can't believe what I read online to the man in front of me. He's every bit as amazing as the articles about him. I ignored the nasty and clearly jealous ones trying to tear him down because he has been nothing short of a gentleman to me.

I take a decent sip of my coffee and lower my cup. "So, I looked you up online last week."

His brow perks, and he leans back, not saying anything, so I speak again. "After your mother said your name, I was like, where do I know him from?" I tap my temple with a smile.

His face is unchanged, but his eyes are slightly widened. "Did I impress you or disgust you?"

My face drops, and I frown. What? "Disgust? Why would you disgust me?"

"Because I come from money."

I stare at him, baffled. "I definitely didn't feel that way. I was overwhelmed but more about how intelligent you are and..." I trail off and he encourages me to continue with a wave of his hand, clearly wanting to discover the rest.

"Curious. Why did you leave your business? You're a billionaire. You invented an app, but then you left. I'm just trying to understand you."

He looks down, and his grip on his coffee cup tightens. His knuckles are white, and then he releases the cup and rests his hands on the table as he gazes back at me. A breath leaves my lungs with relief, not wanting to make him uncomfortable, but isn't this what he wanted? Us to get to know each other?

We lock eyes, and I give him the time he needs to think about an answer. Knowing that if it was me, I would be the same.

"Yes. I invented Integration Software, and my dad succeeded in IT too. So, you could say we both hit it big. But my parents thought they could control me."

I frown, not understanding, but keep quiet.

"Don't get me wrong. I love them. We don't have a bad relationship. I just had a falling out with them over a topic. We don't agree on it. And I refuse to live my life the way they want me to."

I still don't understand, so I ask, "What do you mean? Like...I'd say this is the part I just don't get. What were they trying to get you to do? That made you walk away to become a driver? Hell, you invented Integration Software and then you left that to be a driver. You don't have to work because you're a self-made billionaire, but yet you are James's driver. I'm sorry, I don't get it. I'm just so confused."

He offers me a small smile. "Yes, I have money, but it doesn't mean I don't want to work. I love working hard. And James understands my situation. Hence, why he gave me a job."

I'm about to talk, but he continues, so I close my mouth and listen. "I know you're still trying to figure out why, so even though I don't like to talk about it, I will. For you. We are trying to get to know each other, and well, this is important."

Oh.

"The reason my parents and I had a falling out and why I left the company was because my parents want me to marry a certain person and I don't like or love that person."

He rubs the back of his neck, and I take a sip of coffee, needing to wet my mouth.

"She seems like a nice enough woman, but there's nothing there."

I was not expecting that answer. *His parents want to marry him off.*

"Why can't you choose?"

"They think they know me better and they don't think I'll get married."

My mouth falls in shock. "You don't want to get married?"

"I do."

I take a breath. "Then why didn't you accept?"

He chuckles, and the lightness in him makes me smile.

"It would have been easier," he says, more to himself as he picks up the coffee and drains the cup. "But truthfully, I hadn't found anyone worth marrying so when they brought her around to the house to meet me, it was awkward, and I became furious. I couldn't do it. There's just nothing between us."

"How did the woman feel?" I ask, wondering how I would feel being forced into marriage.

He snorts. "To be honest, she was happy to get married. And she kind of seemed sad when I refused to marry her."

"I wonder why..." I say and put my hand under my chin to listen.

"Did she want to marry me for money? That's probably what you're thinking, but I honestly don't think so, because she came from money. But then what? Why would you want to marry someone you barely know? You can't say you're marrying me for love," he says with a strained laugh before continuing. "I can't trust what the intention of us getting married would be. Because your parents forced you to get married. That's just not enough for me. I need more."

"What's more?" I breathe, suddenly feeling a tightness in my chest from the way he's staring at me.

"I need a connection. I need sparks. I need love. I do want a future...but with the right person."

I swallow hard and neither of us moves; it's dead silent between us, and all I can hear and feel is the beat of my racing heart.

As I think about his words, I check every single one off.

We have a connection.

We have a spark, but I guess we don't have love.

My throat has closed off, and I'm struggling for air as I think about the way I'm feeling toward him.

Could I fall in love with Jonathan Black?

Yes, yes, I could.

John pays for the coffee, and as we walk outside, his phone rings. He moves to the side to answer it. After a couple of minutes of feeling awkward, I walk to Sally's. It's only a short walk. I'll walk fast and at least I can chat with her until John comes inside to meet me.

As I walk, I feel something...that airiness comes back. *You've got to be kidding.*

My heart is racing. I look over my shoulder behind me, but I see nothing. I shake my head and tell myself I'm delirious while quickening my pace. I can't get there quick enough.

"Ruby," a voice calls, and my shoulders relax, because I know this person. Paul is a client. Well, an ex-client. So, I breathe again and smile. I can't believe I panicked over him.

"Hi."

"How are you?" he asks with a glowing smile, standing close in a bomber jacket, black shirt, and cargo pants.

"I'm good. How's everything with you?" I ask, my arms crossed over my chest.

The gleam in his eye causes my relief to quickly fade.

He shrugs with a sly smirk "Same old. I miss you."

Those words.

The same ones on the note.

I miss you...

Panic now rises through my chest, and my heart is beating wildly in my ear. I wonder if I'm in a nightmare and need to wake up.

I force a smile, but it's a stretch, not knowing how to respond to this insane interaction. He misses me? What, as in our therapy sessions where we spoke about his awful upbringing and ways to cope? I don't miss him, and my throat constricts when I remember how he's been asking me out a lot. And I want to kick myself at why didn't I think of ending our sessions after the first time he asked me out. Hindsight is a wonderful thing, but not practical when you're on the verge of a panic attack.

I swallow as I realize the eeriness is still there, and it's stronger. And I feel like all the puzzle pieces are clicking together, but there is that small part of wishful thinking.

He hasn't. He wouldn't.

But as the panic bubbles beneath the surface and rumbles through my body, I know in my gut it's him.

Fuck, this is the guy.

It's him.

Has to be him.

He's been following me.

It all makes sense now. And I close my eyes, sucking in deep breaths, trying to take big lungfuls of air. It's harder through my restricted throat and my damn brain won't switch off, adding to the fear and panic.

He grew fond of me when I was trying to help him sort through his childhood trauma.

He always thought I was an angel, and he used to say I helped him heal and how much he wanted to take me out to thank me. I had to explain recently that I didn't date clients. So, then he left and still kept coming to the clinic to ask me out and I said, *I'm not interested.*

The panic seems to rise, and my breaths quicken.

"Angel, your color is white. Are you okay?" he says as he tries to touch me.

I jump back, struggling to breathe, looking around with wide eyes. Inside, I'm praying that John will come.

I want to get inside, knowing it'll be safer there. I blow out a shaky breath. "Oh, I've got to go get an order. Sally is waiting for me."

I'm wrong. He immediately insists on coming along.

And I panic. I don't want him to keep following me. And I can't say anything to Sally if he stands right beside me.

"I don't think that's a good idea," I say, trying to put on my strongest voice, even though I'm vibrating with nerves.

"Why?" he asks, puzzled.

"I'm not feeling very comfortable."

His brows pinch together. "Why? I care about you. We would be so good together. I can take care of you."

He strokes my arm. And now I'm visibly shaking my teeth, clicking them noisily. I close my mouth and look around before returning to face him.

Oh my god. What the hell am I gonna do?

"Please don't touch me. Have you been following me?"

"Not really," he says and keeps his hand on me.

I try to move, but he mimics my stance.

Reality sets in when his answer confirms it's been him.

"You shouldn't do it. It's been frightening me."

His face falls. "I didn't mean to frighten you. I just wanted to see you."

"I get that, but there'll be nothing between us. Ever."

"Is it because of him?" he spits angrily, and my back straightens.

"Who?"

"The tall, dark-haired guy. He always wears a black suit."

Oh gosh. I know exactly who he means. *John.*

I don't want to tell him John's name, so I brush it off. "I'm single, and I'm not interested in anybody."

"But you won't go on a coffee date with me," he argues in a clipped tone.

And he's right, I won't. I need to get out here so I can call the cops. He's getting angrier now that he's asking about John.

"I'm gonna go into Sally's now and get my flowers. I think it's time for you to go home."

"I don't want to go home. I want to be with you." He squeezes my arm, and I try to shake off his grip, but his hand is too tight.

"You can't, and please stop following me." The back of my eyes sting with tears and the last words come out pleading.

"You heard her."

I close my eyes, and a tear of relief falls when I hear John's voice.

"That's him," Paul says.

"Take. Your. Hand. Off. Her," John says venomously. I can hear the shake in his voice. "Now!"

Paul drops it fast and steps back. Having John's presence around me makes me relax a little. I'm so grateful right now. I'm still shaken, but in the corner of my eye, I can see a police car.

I wonder if John called them or if it was an onlooker. Either way I'm grateful.

I blow out a breath and wipe my eyes roughly with the back of my hands, refusing to cry.

Paul spots the police and tries to make a run for it, screaming, "I haven't done anything."

I bury my face in my hands as my heart beats faster. This is a disaster. I've never given him a sign we would ever be anything. I was there for him, treating him, helping him through trauma.

And it seems he's grown attached.

It's hard not to feel guilty and mull over our sessions. Like have I said or done anything that would give him this impression? I've heard of this happening, but this is the first time it's happened to me.

"Come here," John commands, and he turns with wide open arms.

I grab his middle, resting my head on his chest, hearing his thumping heartbeats. He wraps his arms around me, so I tighten mine and cuddle him back.

He feels like relief. And it's what I need. He's exactly what I need. The only person I want touching me.

He's always there when I need him.

"Thank you," I mumble into his solid chest, taking a deep inhale of his scent.

Masculine, fresh and calming.

After a couple of minutes of holding each other, he asks, "You okay?"

Am I? Honestly, I don't know.

I shake my head, unable to speak.

"I have an idea," he says.

"Mm?"

"How about we go to Sally's? James can suck it; you're more important. And I'll take you to your grandma's house?"

I think about his offer, and I remain silent, soaking in the information.

"I don't think you're in the right frame of mind to drive right now."

"But what about the cops?"

"I'll deal with it. And they can follow us to her house if needed. But at the moment, I think you need comfort and your grandma."

I nod as my heart swells. "Thank you. That's exactly what I need right now."

However, I'm not ready to disconnect from his arms.

He takes the choice away from me and steps back but takes my hand. "Come on. Let's get this over with."

"James is gonna be mad at you," I say as we step inside Sally's.

"I don't care. You're more important."

I can't help but be happy to hear that.

Walking through the flower shop, holding his hand, looks like we are together, but I'm not letting his hand go.

Sally turns at the sound of us walking through and watches us with a raised eyebrow. Her eyes dart between us. "Ruby. John. How nice to see you. Ready to pick up your orders?"

"Yes," I say before John takes over to talk to Sally.

"I need you to send mine as a delivery this week for James's order."

Sally nods and says, "Sure thing, just tell me the address and I'll arrange for delivery today."

He rattles off the address and gives her money for the delivery.

"Can I have my usual saffron order?" I ask quietly.

"You don't sound like yourself, Ruby. Is everything okay?" She leans forward with a concerned expression.

"Not really, but I will be. I just can't explain it today."

"Oh, no problem. Just that you look pale."

I cough out a laugh.

John squeezes my hand. "Are you okay?"

"No. I'm fine."

His stare is intense, as if reading every line on my face.

"I promise." To assure him, I try to crack a smile.

He nods and pulls me into him, embracing my shoulders. I wrap my arm around his waist, his body covering me and offering the comfort I need to calm down from the state of shock I've found myself in.

This is nice. This is really nice.

Sally hands me the saffron, and we leave the shop, leaving her wondering what's going on between us. To be honest, I don't know how I could answer that, because I don't have any idea what we're doing.

Jonathan

Paul is arrested and taken away. Grabbing Ruby's hand, I walk her toward my car. She is indeed pale, and I don't want her driving home in a state of shock. I can't imagine what she must be feeling to have someone follow, and even worse...to be an ex-client.

I feel this deep, protective nature coming out of me. The way I vibrated with anger when he had his hand on her and she asked him to remove it, yet the bastard left it on; I have never wanted to hit someone so much in my life. But I'm better than that. I can threaten him with my words and not embarrass her by having a news article about me hitting her stalker. No, I must keep myself in check and remember I'm here to support her. I just want to wrap her in my arms tonight and make sure she won't be threatened again.

"What's going to happen to my car?" she asks and her sweet voice pulls me away from my thoughts.

"I'll sort it out," I say and squeeze her a little tighter, reminding her I'm here for her. And that she will not have to worry about anything again. I want to help any way I can. All she needs to do is relax.

"You don't have to keep saving me." She peeks up at me from under her lashes, and I smile down.

It's an effort to stop myself from kissing her, so instead, I speak, "I want to help you. Please let me. And let's just get to your grandma's and we can worry about it later."

She nods, giving up the fight, and we get into the car.

After a quiet drive, I park outside the house. My palms sweat as I realize I'm meeting her family. I haven't met anyone's parents in years.

Getting out of the car, I walk around to her side and grab her hand to go toward the door.

She peers up and holds my gaze with a smirk. "Are you ready to meet Flora?"

"Always." I give her my charming smirk and then we step through the door.

"Grandma," she says as we walk in, and I close it behind us.

"Yeah. Come in. I'm in the kitchen," Flora says.

"Okay, well, I have someone with me," Ruby yells out.

"Is he handsome?" she asks.

I pinch my lips together to prevent myself from laughing. Ruby's face isn't pale anymore. No, there is definitely a change of color to her now, and if I can read her correctly, I'd say she thinks I am.

"How do you know it's a *he*?" Ruby challenges.

"I just do," Flora fires back.

We turn a corner, making our way to a kitchen.

Flora blurts, "Oh, fuck me silly. He's delicious."

My lips part, and I can't help but chuckle even though when I peer down at Ruby, she's frowning, clearly unimpressed. "Grandma."

She's probably five feet tall and is grinning from ear to ear as if butter wouldn't melt in her mouth. She swears like a sailor and seems to have zero filter.

Not knowing the proper etiquette, I offer my hand to shake, but she shakes her head and yanks on my arm until I step closer to her, and she plants a kiss on each cheek. I pull back and she squeezes both of my cheeks. "These look like the only ounce of fat on you."

"Oh. My. God," Ruby mumbles, mortified.

"What? He's handsome," Flora says with a shrug, not understanding the issue.

"Not the only reason he's here," Ruby reminds her. "He's smart and caring too."

That makes my heart thump harder; the fact she's the only woman who sees past the money and my looks. I feel blessed to have met her. I may have to thank James for making me buy flowers, otherwise I'd never have met her. And what a sad fucking thought that is.

"My granddaughter is so lucky. But you are too because she is my favorite granddaughter."

"I'm your only granddaughter, so say that!" Ruby laughs and I can't help but join her too.

"Well, that's true. Now, did you bring the saffron for the pie?"

I hold it up and wave it. "We sure did. And I cannot wait to taste it."

"Well, you're in for a treat, handsome."

"Grandma, he has a name, and it's John," Ruby says, clearly annoyed.

I smile, watching this exchange, wishing my grandparents were still around. They definitely weren't as out there as Ruby's, but they were warm and kind too.

"Let's cook the pie and then we can sit and have some tea while the pie bakes."

"Sounds good. How can I help?" I offer.

"And he wants to cook. Listen, Ruby, if you don't marry him, I will." She winks at me, and I bite back a chuckle because Ruby has stiffened uncomfortably.

"No one is marrying anyone," Ruby retorts.

I'm not ready to marry right now, either. But dating? Hell yes. And if she doesn't agree to the date like I have planned, then I'll be gutted. I want to take her out and bring a smile back on her face...and maybe kiss that sweet face.

Yeah, definitely that.

Even now, as I stand here waiting to receive my instruction on how I can help, my gaze keeps straying to those pink lips. I've never wanted to kiss someone so much in my life.

"If you're going to offer, I'll need your muscles to do the mixing. Ruby, can you make the tea?"

"Sure." She moves away from me to make the tea, and I join Flora behind the counter and follow her directions.

As I help her, I look out the corner of my eye, catching glimpses of Ruby moving around.

"Do you want tea, or would you prefer coffee?" Ruby asks.

"The usual, sweetheart," Flora responds.

Ruby shakes her head. "I meant John."

I smirk. "I'd love a coffee. Black, no sugar or cream."

"How do you drink that? It's so bland." Flora tsks.

"I'm used to it."

The old woman doesn't say anything else, just puts the mix into the cake pan.

"Take a seat at the table," Flora says.

"I'll help clean up," I offer.

Flora lays a hand on her chest and widens her eyes. "I don't know if you're going to give me a heart attack or an orgasm first."

I chuckle loudly, taken aback by her. How do I answer that?

"Have you had a drink today? You're being a little extra," Ruby says from the table where she's blowing the steam coming from her cup.

I take a seat to join her at the table, and she mouths, *I'm so sorry.*

I smile and mouth back, *It's okay.*

"Nope. Only water and tea, sweetheart."

Thirty minutes later a knock sounds at the door, and a woman's voice filters in. "Mom, it's just us."

"Oh goodie, you will love them," Flora says excitedly, and I look at Ruby, whose slack mouth and stilled body cause me to feel a little sorry for her. I don't even have to guess this is her parents.

And holy fuck. I'm about to meet the parents. Well, this is a lot for one day.

I turn when the footsteps stop behind me, then smile and stand.

"Oh, hi," Ruby's mom says, her eyes flicking to Grandma and Ruby before returning to mine. "I wasn't expecting anyone else."

"Don't worry. Neither was I, but this is Ruby's *friend*," Flora explains, but the way she said *friend*, it's clear she isn't buying it. But I'm glad she chose not to lose herself and make any other comments.

"Mom, Dad, this is Jonathan. John, these are my parents, Hugh and Pearl."

I shake their hands and they both smile warmly at me, and we exchange greetings. I peer over at Ruby, who's staring wide-eyed and now has a flushed face, probably overwhelmed now. So, I decide it's time for me to leave and let her calm down from the big day. I can't imagine how hard today's been, and having me meet the parents without warning is another layer added to her stressful day.

"I should be going now. But it was so lovely to meet you all," I say.

"You haven't had the cake yet," Flora says.

The oven timer goes off just then. "How about I take a piece home?"

"That I can do." Flora turns and grabs the cake from the oven and cuts me a large piece.

After I say goodbye to everyone, Ruby walks me out. We stay silent until we step out onto the porch, keeping the door closed behind us.

My gaze moves to the window beside us. "Do you think your grandma is watching us through the curtain?"

She laughs and turns to look at the window too. "Probably. And thanks again for everything. I couldn't have done this without you."

"Anytime. I'm glad I could be there to help. Now it may not be the greatest time to ask, but I'll regret it if I don't."

"Mm."

"I think it's time for us to go on a proper date. Don't you think?"

She nibbles on her lip, before saying, "Yeah, that would be amazing."

"Well, I'll text you later and see how you're feeling. You seem okay...but are you, really?" I ask as I grab her upper arm, unable to resist touching her. I hold her gaze, waiting for her to answer.

She nods. "Yes. I promise I would have told you if I wasn't. He'll be all right. He's in safe hands."

I frown, not liking how she's thinking of him and worried about him. I couldn't care less about him. "Hey, don't worry about him. You worry about yourself. He scared you."

She appears sad for a moment. "I know, I just...worry about him too."

"You don't know that," I say, horrified she isn't seeing the seriousness of the situation. There isn't anything harmless about him. But I guess this is the person she is. Caring, compassionate, and kind. A way better person than me.

"True," she mumbles.

She needs to stop thinking about today and go rest. "Go back inside with your parents and your grandma, and I'll speak to you later."

I kiss her on the cheek and leave her standing on the porch, smiling. I cannot wait for the date.

JONATHAN

Ruby: How formal is this date? I don't know how to dress. Should I wear jeans or a dress?

John: Whatever you feel comfortable in :)

Ruby: Ugh, that doesn't help! Can you just tell me where we're going?

John: Nope. Just worry about impressing me, and know that I'm already impressed.

Ruby: Aren't you sweet? But thanks for not helping. I guess I'll have to go back to trying on all my clothes and finding the ones I like...

John: You're welcome to send pics if you need help ;)

Ruby: For not helping me, you can see what I choose when you come to pick me up.

John: Cheeky. But if you change your mind, I'm happy to help. Otherwise, I'll see you in an hour.

Ruby: Counting down the minutes.

John: So am I.

KNOCKING ON HER DOOR mimics the thumping of my heart. Who would have thought you could be nervous to see someone you spoke to earlier in the day and saw only a week ago? But text messaging her every day has brought us closer. So close now, only a door stands between us. A gush of air leaves my lungs when she opens the door. She looks breathtaking.

Tension leaves me as soon as a smile erupts on her face and she says, "I'm glad I chose the dress."

"Same. You look exquisite," I say as I run my eyes over her tight-fitting black dress, which hugs her curves and makes me feel even more grateful she agreed to this date. Her heels add to her height too, bringing her eyes closer to mine, letting me barely tilt my head and be able to kiss her…cheek. Even if I want to kiss her lips, I don't. Instead, I lean down and kiss her cheek and take a deep inhale of her perfume…or is it her shampoo? Her hair is down and curly, and I want to run my fingers through it. But that's for another time or later if she wants to. But for right now, I take her hand and then we drive to the restaurant.

We step inside the dimly lit restaurant. I peer at her, and she's beaming. I turn back and talk to the waitress who escorts us to our seats. The low jazz music playing through the speakers is soft and sets the mood. I've never been here because I haven't wanted to take anyone here, but Ruby is special, and this place is exactly for these dates. We pass a large single chandelier in the center. And the mix of mirror and soft cream walls catches Ruby's attention. We take our seats in old fashioned curved gray fabric chairs, and the waitress hands us a menu before pouring water and leaving us alone. I lean back in my chair, grinning at my date, who's smiling back at me with equal enthusiasm.

"This place is beautiful. I never knew this existed," she says, taking in every inch of the place.

"It is. I've never been here, but I've heard the best things."

"You haven't come here before?"

"No. There hasn't been anyone in my life in years, which is why my parents are trying to marry me off," I say with a chuckle, but her expression drops.

I wonder if she forgot about that. I wish I could, but it's my life they are trying to control.

Thankfully, the waitress comes and asks us what we want to drink. Ruby scans the menu before choosing a wine, and I order the bottle for us to share.

"Do you think you'll ever give in and marry who they choose?" she asks, and I wonder if this has been playing on her mind. Like, is she a toy in this? Am I going to have a date and walk back to marrying my parents' choice? Hell no!

I shake my head. "Never. They actually don't care who it is...well, within reason, but they want the image of me settled down and married with kids on the way."

She blinks and takes a sip of her water.

"It's okay. I'm not going to ask you to marry me tomorrow and have my babies."

She leans back into the chair, and I chuckle before saying, "But if I had my choice. It'll be you."

"Oh." She blinks, looking down at the table and then back at me with a tinge to her cheeks.

"There is something that has drawn me to you, and I know I've never experienced the feelings I have for you with anyone else. So, if I can tell my parents who my future is with, I'm going to say your name, Ruby. It might seem forward, but I haven't waited thirty-five years to meet my other half to just let her go and not say a word. No. You deserve my honesty."

Our eyes clash, swirling with unbridled emotions, and her chest moves up and down. I don't say anything else; I give her the space to digest and breathe.

The waitress comes when she's about to speak, so she closes her mouth and picks up her glass of wine and we toast before she takes a big sip. We order food before continuing our conversation.

"That was deep, and I'm totally lost for words, so just give me a second to find the right ones," she says with a warm smile.

"You don't need perfect words. I just want to know how you feel."

Holding her glass in her hand, she looks at me with a new smile. It reaches her eyes and shows her lines of maturity, and I want to know what she is thinking right now. I'm tapping my foot under the table impatiently, but I can't hurry her. No, she needs to do this in her time, and I hope I get what I desperately want to hear; I'm her future and she chooses me. And finally, I'll get my future of having a wife I love.

But even if tonight is all that she'll give me, then I'll take it, but I'm hoping she sees a future with me too.

"I'm not getting any younger either, and I have a career I've dreamed about and while it's fulfilled me, I still feel lonely," she says with a laugh, but it's strained, and I know it's to cover the pain. But what pain? I need to know, so I sit here, unmoving, and let her continue talking.

"I go home to my empty house and I want to tell someone about my day."

"What about when you go to parties like engagements or weddings, and they give you a plus one, but you don't have one?" I add to her thoughts.

"And you go alone, pretending you're okay, but deep down, you wish you could find your person like them," she says with a sigh, but there is an intensity in her gaze that matches mine.

"I also haven't been this attracted to another being. It scares me," she whispers.

I swallow, knowing what she means. "It scares me too."

We stay silent for a beat.

"But I guess you've met my family already." She breaks the silence.

"And you've met my mother, but you haven't met the rest. Oh, when my mother discovers you're my girlfriend, I'm sure you'll see a different side." I laugh.

"I don't know whether to be relieved or worried." She smirks.

I see the waitress coming back for our meal order, so I say, "You'll be fine," before she interrupts.

"Will you go back and work for your business?" She swirls the noodles on her fork, and I watch her eat it. And damn, she is so seductive when she eats.

"Well, I've been playing around with a new app. And I should thank you."

She frowns. "What?"

"It's about security after what you went through. It's in the planning stage, so I don't know all the details, but when I have them all, I'd love to run them past you."

She blinks rapidly and softly shakes her head, as if clearing it.

I frown and ask, "What was that for?"

"You're so smart. I seriously don't think I've met a guy who invents anything or is driven to do his own thing." She chokes on a laugh, and it makes me smile. It's nice knowing I impress her with my brains and not my wallet.

"You're smart too." I wink.

"Thanks. But you have more than enough money and you don't have to work, but the passion and drive to keep working are sexy."

I raise a brow at her. She thinks of me as sexy. "I'm definitely passionate and driven when I want something."

My double meaning isn't lost on her, and the way her neck flushes makes me want to put my mouth on her and feel how warm her skin is.

Ruby

HAVE YOU EVER BEEN pulled in a different direction? Well, as we are driving home, I can't help but feel the energy between us hit another level. Intimate, hot, charged. This is the feeling suffocating me.

Is he feeling it too?

His green top and dark jeans show off his strong body. John's eyes are on the road. His expression is unchanged, but when I look over his hands grip the steering wheel with white-knuckled force, I wonder if just maybe he's feeling the same intense desire. The ache between my legs is uncomfortable, so I squeeze my thighs together to relieve the pain, but it's still there. I turn and look out the window, figuring the best thing to do is to ignore it and hope it goes away.

When we arrive at the house, my heart skips a beat. I grip my bag and go through the motion in my head—say thanks for a good evening, then go inside the house. Sounds simple enough.

But when I stand on my porch, wringing my hands together and staring into his eyes, getting lost in them, the words, "Would you like to come inside?" slip out.

Oops.

A large smile erupts on his face, and the glow from the porch light shows the lines around his eyes, making my stomach twist and tumble with nerves. A sexy guy is about to be in my house with no one else around and my bedroom not too far away. But instead of nerves, there's a giddiness I've never felt before. The thrill of never having such a deep connection to a guy tells me how much I like him. He cares for me, likes me, and sees a future with me. What guy talks about marriage so openly? But for him, it was as easy as breathing. When he talks, I feel every single word he says down to my core. And the little flutter and tingle running through me let me know I feel everything back as hard.

"Is there saffron cake?" he asks with an arched brow.

His question makes me smile. "You're in luck because usually, I'd have eaten it all by now."

"I am lucky." The words are bold, and I bite my lip at his double meaning. He doesn't hold back on complimenting me. It's refreshing and brazen, and if he doesn't stop, I'll rip his clothes off.

I clear my throat and open my door, feeling his presence heating my back. I give a brief tour on the way to the kitchen, purposefully not telling him where my bedroom is. It's not that I don't want that...because I do! It's just if he's in my room, I know I'll kiss him. The more he's in my space, the further he creeps under my skin and into my heart. Having some cake and talking will give us both a breather to make sure we want to take the next step. I know that's what I want, and I'm proud that I'm holding back, giving him the option. It doesn't have to happen tonight; there's plenty of time.

I put the plate with the cake and two forks on the counter between us.

He says, "Thanks," then digs straight in. He groans, and it's so deep and guttural that I cough on the piece I just shoveled into my mouth. He opens my cupboard, looking for a glass, and grabs water from the fridge, offering it to me to stop my coughing.

"Thanks," I say when I can talk again without feeling like another coughing fit will come.

"This cake is so good. But it can be dangerous. I saw the ingredients, and it's not healthy," he teases.

"Yeah, I should really not be having it weekly."

He narrows his eyes at me and shakes his head. "No, eat it. I love your shape." He uses his fork to grab another bite-sized piece and holds it out to my lips. I'm heating up as we hold each other's gaze, and I lick my lips before I open my mouth and let him feed me.

I watch him as I chew, and his eyes darken. He nods before taking another bite for me, but I grab the fork and turn it to him, and there's a small lift to the corner of his lips before he opens his mouth. He groans. It's so deep and sexy, I feel it in my core. God, I got the vision of him between my thighs, groaning and eating me. The hunger in his eyes should be for me and not the stupid cake. I want him, and he wants me. So, what the fuck am I doing eating cake right now? When I could have a mouth full of him, or better yet, his mouth on me.

I step toward him and pull his head to mine so I can crash my lips into his. He doesn't falter, instead he grunts loudly, making me crazy. The kiss turns to teeth clashing, hands touching, tongues tangling, and neither of us can get enough of the other. The taste of saffron and his warm tongue dancing with mine is the best damn kiss I've ever had, and when I step back, my body hits the counter. His frame is flushed to mine. I feel his thick hard cock against my stomach, and it causes a heaviness to hit my sex. If he were to touch me now, he'd find me wet.

His hands grab my head, tilting mine, and he kisses me as if this is the only night we've been given. There has been too much passion and emotion swirling between us in the last few weeks, so now it's all coming out. He grunts again and my thighs quiver, the anticipation almost causing tears to form. I haven't been with someone in a long time and this passion is something I've missed. But this connection, though...I've never had this before and I bet with one touch, I'd crumble.

Our kiss slows, so we can catch our breath. I inhale his scent, and he does the same. The swap in the air adds to my already intoxicated state; I'm drunk on him. I only had two glasses tonight with dinner, so that has disappeared, but he now consumes me.

He pulls back, but I keep my eyes closed, sucking in fresh air and waiting for the next kiss. "You're so sweet, and the mix of cake and you is a damn lethal combination." The touch on my lip from one of his fingers dusting along my bottom lip is causing me to not be able to think anything rational. I can only wonder how I can spread cake over my body and beg him to eat it off me.

"Mm," I mumble incoherently.

He keeps his finger running softly over it as if he's fascinated by it. I stay upright, thankfully, from being wedged between the counter and him, but when he lifts me unexpectedly, I squeak, opening my eyes from the sudden movement. The cold counter on my body and the loss of contact cause me to shiver.

I wrap my legs around his middle and bring my sex flush against his bulge. "This is a better angle."

His face splits into the sexiest smile. "Much better. But it would be even better with you naked, laid out on this counter."

"Well, what's stopping you?" I say, encouraging him to devour me. I want him so much I'd have resorted to begging.

Jonathan

"Nothing, babe. Nothing at all," I say, enjoying how her legs are locked behind my back. The tight friction of her sex on my cock is perfect. The position keeps us close, and I welcome her breath on my face. Her sexy pants are urging me on, and I look over her black dress I'm about to remove. My hands rest on her thighs, skimming them up to her hips where the dress bunches.

She moves off one side, letting me push it over her ass. Her black lacy panties are now peeking through, and a deep growl leaves my chest.

I capture her lips in a kiss, unable to hold back. She whimpers when I pull away, but I want more. Pulling away, I look at the dress and hold it up over her breasts. She lifts her arms, and I take it off and toss it away, leaving her in only a black set. The delicate lace complements her skin, and my dick pulses at the sight.

"John," she pants.

I smirk. "I know, babe. Soon."

She whines, and I chuckle.

Rather than torturing us anymore, I move my hand to her shoulders and slip the bra off. Then reach around to remove it completely. Her breasts drop and her pebbled nipples are delectable. I bend down and suck one into my mouth, while my other hand squeezes the neglected breast.

She arches into me. "Oh god, yes."

I twirl my tongue around her nipple and suck and squeeze simultaneously, moving a little faster and squeezing a little tighter, and she arches further. I pull away from her nipple with a pop, grazing my teeth along it.

She's lost to the ecstasy, but I want more.

I *need* more.

"Babe, lie down."

Her eyes snap open, and she's flushed. But she nods and quickly obeys. She tilts her head so she can see what I have in mind.

I grab the sides of her panties and pull them down until they drop to the floor. I pause a moment and smile at her. "You're so beautiful."

I run my gaze over her curves, appreciating everything about her. I part her legs wider, and her core makes me suck in a breath. So wet and ready for me.

My heart thunders in my chest. I skim my hands along her inner thighs and they quiver under me.

"So responsive."

"God, yes."

I can't wait to have her writhe under me. I move one hand from the crease of her hip to touch her above the clit, and she cries out, but I don't stop. I move my hands to dust them over her clit and down past her wet core.

"More," she cries.

"I know you want to come so badly, don't you?"

She moans, "Yes."

"I can see you're wet."

She moans again. And I repeat the motion but stop at her opening and gently push in one finger. She tries to close her leg, but I push it open again, needing to watch my finger in her. I continue, but need more, so I add another finger.

As soon as I insert the second finger, she says, "Yes, that's it."

So, I curl my fingers along her wall on the way out, finding her spot where I need to focus my attention on. When I hit it, her head tips back and she moans.

It's so hard standing here and holding myself back. I badly want to lean forward and taste her, but I want her first orgasm on my hand so I can take my time when I eat her.

My thumb hits her clit and I rub circles. Her walls clamp down. I keep up the pace as she writhes and moans. I flick my gaze between my fingers and her flushed face, and she's so beautiful I want to watch both, but it's impossible.

I watch my fingers until she quivers and tilts her head back further, crumbling from the orgasm wracking through her body. I don't stop until her back hits the counter, and she flutters her eyes open and tries to catch her breath.

"Feel better?" I ask with a lopsided grin.

"Much."

"There's much more to come." My voice is deep and full of my own want.

She rises up on her elbows, squinting at me, probably wondering what I mean.

"What about you?"

"I'll let you have me after I get another orgasm from you."

Her face glows at the news. "Oh, really?"

"Yes. Starting right now."

I squat down and bring my mouth down on her, kissing her clit. It's delicate and soft and I press a kiss against her, which causes her skin to cover in goosebumps. I kiss it one more time before I lick her clit and then massage it with my tongue.

"Oh," she murmurs, and I peer up at her without moving my tongue, and I glimpse her still watching me. I move my mouth lower and lick her pussy deep and rub my face against the rest of her pussy, inhaling her scent. Her legs try to close, so I move my hand to her crease. I'm totally fine with being suffocated in her pussy. She tastes and smells like heaven, and I'm glad I got her first orgasm out already.

I continue licking her, each time getting inside a little deeper. Her hand pushes into my hair, and I lift off slightly to see her chest rising and falling, her lust-filled eyes watching me, but it's her parted lips that have me smiling broadly. She looks fucked, and I haven't even started. I move back to lick and kiss her pussy, and she grips my hair tighter.

"I don't think I could ever have enough of your sweet pussy."

"Oh God."

Her hips grind my face, and I fucking love it. Her pussy feels so good, and with each move, I thrust my tongue inside.

I insert two of my digits inside her and simultaneously move my mouth to her clit. She arches up. I can't give her anymore. I move my fingers faster and bite down a little harder on her clit, and she convulses.

"Oh, John, Joh—"

Her moans are everything. The way she says my name makes me wild. I can't wait to fuck her. I keep up what I'm doing until her body slacks, and I disconnect my mouth and pull out my fingers and stand. Her eyes flutter open, and she looks at me with a fucked look in her eyes. And my chest swells with happiness and pride.

She's sucking in deep breaths, and I keep my gaze locked on her while I remove my top. She nibbles on her lips, and it makes my balls tighten. She's so damn sexy I can't wait to fuck her.

I remove my pants and briefs, and I watch her lip pop out, and she swallows hard, still panting. My cock is out, and she's fucking looking at it like she wants to feast on it. But even though I want to slip my cock between her lips, I want to fuck her pussy more. I want to feel her around me. I grab my wallet and roll on a condom.

I bring her body down a little, so she's off the counter and giving me better access to fuck her...hard.

"Are you ready?" I ask, holding my cock in my hand, ready to line her up.

My other hand is holding her hip on the edge of the counter. I'm shaking, holding back, waiting for her to answer.

"Yes. Hell yes."

I chuckle. "Well, let's not keep you waiting."

I push the tip into her, and her pussy grips me like a vice. So tight. I close my eyes and take deep breaths, needing to calm down my racing heart. The adrenaline is too much and the way my balls are drawing up into my body, I know it wants to fucking come. And it can't. I want to get another orgasm out of her. Thrusting further causes my hand to grip her hip tight.

"Fuck, Ruby. This is so good."

"Mm."

"Those fucking noises and your sweet pussy accepting me is so fucking good."

"Ohhh." The mix of her moans and the sound of our skin slapping each other in her kitchen is beyond any of my wildest dreams. There's a passion so strong that I don't know if I can hold back any longer. I lean over and grip the counter with one hand, but I leave the other still gripping her hip while I thrust deep into her. She grabs on to my shoulder, and I hope I can hold on long enough to feel her orgasm on me.

I thrust hard a few more times before I lean back and grab one leg, lifting it onto my shoulder. I push inside her again, and at this angle, I hit in deeper.

The way she tightens around me causes me to grunt. "Fuck. Please tell me you're close. I—"

"I'm close."

Thank fuck!

I thrust harder, and I'm holding back with everything I can. My body sweats, causing her leg to slip, but I hold it with my hand and thrust.

I can't hold on any longer. I groan as the orgasm hits, and she moans, and the way her muscles contract, I know she is too.

I continue to fuck her until she's spent and then I lower her leg and scoop her off the counter and whisper, "Where's your room?"

Her head stays burrowed in the crook of my shoulder. She points, and I follow her into a simple modern bedroom. It's fresh, calm and so her.

I pull back the white covers and lie her down and kiss her lips and say, "I'll be back."

I discard the condom in the bathroom and slip into the bed beside her. She snuggles into my chest. The feeling is so heavenly. I know I'll have the best damn sleep tonight; after all, she's here, safe.

And mine.

All mine.

Ruby

Five weeks later

I push the red meat around my plate, trying not to vomit. I'm swallowing the excess saliva that's building in my mouth, trying to eat, but I'm so damn nauseated. We're at his parents' place for dinner. Since we started dating, John and his parents have been slowly repairing their relationship. It's still a work in progress but with our new Sunday night tradition it's moving in the right direction. I usually love our weekly catch-up, however tonight, all I want to do is bail.

"Ruby, is everything all right? You look pale and you haven't eaten much," Monica asks with a wrinkle between her brows.

I swallow hard, pushing the bile back into my stomach. I muster up a fake smile and then say with a slight wobble in my voice, "Yes, Mrs. Black. I'm fine, just lost in thought, sorry."

With her cutlery poised in her hands, she leans forward, wearing a worried expression for a moment before her face softens and she says, "First, please call me Monica. My last name makes me feel old. And I hope everything is okay. Is it your grandmother or work troubles?"

I blink and peer down at my plate for a second. What the hell do I say to that? Both would be a lie, but I'll have to say a little white lie until I figure out what's really wrong with me.

I clear my throat and glance back up at her face. John grabs my hand and squeezes it, pulling my gaze to him.

"I'm fine. Just work, that's all. It's a bit busy, and I'm just thinking I might need a break soon."

John makes a sound in his throat and whispers, "That sounds amazing."

And I stop the blush from creeping on my face by looking at his mom and reminding myself where we are. I know what John's holiday plan would involve and normally I'd be on his lap asking for a taste, but right now, between being at dinner at his parents' and the nausea rolling in my gut, I couldn't think of anything worse right about now.

A few hours later, I'm pacing my bathroom, holding a damn pregnancy stick I picked up yesterday. Waiting three minutes feels like forever. The pain in my chest is excruciating. This is too soon...

Does he want a baby?

Will he be happy?

I can't even imagine how he'll react. I haven't processed the idea; I can't allow myself to believe it's true until I see the positive line for myself.

Then, and only then, will I decide how I'll break the news.

I grip the pregnancy stick in one hand and the other touches my lower stomach. The bloating and intense senses could be my incoming period, but nausea—no, that's something else.

I haven't told this to John because I want to know for certain. So, I brought the test from the pharmacy, and now my future will be determined by what I read in...two minutes.

Oh God!

Two minutes.

Yes, we're dating, but we don't live together. We spend Saturday night and Sunday together. Therefore, neither of us is ready for a baby, but I guess is anyone ever ready? You'll never have enough time, or enough money, but you'll have enough love for the baby and that's all they need. I could give love and so could John. It's clear enough—his adoration, kindness, and passion toward me. He'd be a devoted dad, but it's only been just over a month, and now...this? This could change our world forever. For better or for worse.

What will it mean for my job? I still enjoy working, and I don't see myself giving it up. But if I'm pregnant, that would mean either I pause my career, or the baby goes to day-care while I work.

John's started drafting his app concept called Safe Host. He's been working so hard on it, taking all his days and even the nights, but I can't complain when I stare into his eyes and there is a newfound spark in him. How will a baby affect that? Rushing to the toilet, I drop to my knees and grip the lid. Vomit threatens to expel, but after a few deep, controlled breaths, I swallow the bile that threatens to spill. This is all too much to think about, but I can't run away. I'm not a coward. I can be scared and nervous, but I can do this. I can do anything, and I need to remember that.

I stand up and check the time.

One minute...

The pacing begins again, and my breath is rapidly increasing, and suddenly I'm becoming dizzy. I stop pacing and lower the test on the sink and step back, staring at myself in the mirror. I'm pale with sweat beads forming. I wash my face with cold water, wanting to calm down my quivering body.

It's time.

I hold my breath and step over to where it sits on the sink.

It's positive.

I crouch down to the floor and let the tears fall. I cannot stop them, and I won't. I need them all out before I speak to John.

When I stop crying, I pick myself up off the floor and have a shower. I want to feel fresh and ready to tell my boyfriend I'm pregnant. And even the thought I'm pregnant after we've only been together for a month makes tears fall again. *This is too soon.*

Standing under the stream, I tip my head back and enjoy the warm water on my face. I stay under until the water runs cold and I'm numb.

After the shower, I text John. I want it off my chest and into the open as soon as possible. The best part of our relationship is the honesty we share, and I'm not breaking that now.

He's the best thing to happen, and I was certain we were on a path leading to a future together. Will this change anything? Will he run away?

Ruby: Can you come over?

John: Yeah, why? Is everything okay?

Ruby: I'll explain when you come. See you soon. x

When the knock on the door comes, I feel like my heartbeat is in my throat and I don't know if I'm sick with nerves or I'm about to vomit from the morning sickness. Briefly closing my eyes, I suck in a deep breath and expel it before opening the door.

I try to smile, but it doesn't feel natural. Usually, he's the best part of my day and I smile whenever he's around. But I'm too emotional, and I want this conversation over so I can deal with whatever the next step is. It's hard to do the most basic things when your mind keeps replaying the practiced conversations of how this will play out. But thankfully, he doesn't notice. He steps inside and kisses me. I sigh into his lips. When he pulls away, I close the door and follow him into the kitchen.

He sits on a stool and asks, "What's up?"

I gaze up into his eyes, and the concern in them is too much, so I look down at the counter. Talking to it rather than him seems a better option, but his eyes make me feel too much and I'm trying to hold back. "Did you want a drink?"

"No, thanks. I want to know what's wrong," he says, and the concern in his voice causes the back of my eyes to sting. And a fresh new set of tears sits on my lashes. Who would have thought I could cry this much?

"I...Ah...We—" I swallow the lump in my throat and say in a rush, "We're having a baby."

His eyes are wide, and the shock is evident on his face.

"What? That's not what I was expecting."

"What did you think?"

"I thought you were breaking things off, and I was about to convince you not to."

I shake my head and the tears roll down my cheeks as I whisper, "Never."

He slips off the stool and stands in front of me. He lays his hands on either side of my cheeks and I melt into them. Enjoying his warmth on me, soaking in the comfort of him.

He smiles. "You're pregnant for real?"

I laugh. "Yes, for real, the stick is in the bathroom."

"Show me," he says and drops his hands from my cheeks. I instantly miss his touch. But I frown at his words.

And he's quick to grab my hands and say, "It's not I don't believe you. It's that I want to see it."

I understand what he means. As if seeing the stick with the positive sign will make it more real.

I follow him into the bathroom. He grabs the stick while I stay in the doorway. He peers down, and I can't see his face to get a read on him.

He clutches it in his hand and then turns; his eyes glossy. And he has my heart right here, willing to show me his real emotions, not holding back.

"We're having a baby."

He's not mad...he's happy?

I nod and tears fall. Hard. I cover my face with my hands.

"Oh, babe. Come here."

I wipe the tears roughly with my fingers as I say, "Stupid pregnancy emotions."

He wraps me in his arms, and I snuggle deep into his chest. I want to take a moment to absorb his solace. After a few minutes, the tears stop, and I sniffle, feeling my heartbeat slow down, almost matching the sound of his.

"A baby," he whispers in awe.

Lifting my head, I ask, "Are you okay about it?"

"This isn't your fault. We always use protection, but it's not guaranteed. They break. It happens," he says with a shrug before continuing. "But I'm excited to have a baby with you. My life couldn't be more perfect, and I thank you for that. When we met, I didn't have any direction for my future. I was working and living on autopilot. But the way things have transformed since we got together...You and this baby are my future."

I smile, and he leans forward, capturing my lips in the most tender of kisses. I link my hands behind his neck and kiss him back.

When we pull apart, I whisper, "I guess we need to find a place together."

"Fuck, yeah. Sleeping with you every night will be heaven."

"Don't get excited. Have you seen a pregnancy pillow before?"

He frowns. "No. It's a pillow. How bad can it be?"

I smirk. I won't tell him it's a cock-blocker. I guess when the time is right, he'll see just what this "pillow" does.

The End.

If you want a little extra of John and James as Dad's click here and read it now.

Do you want to read the next friend in the Gentlemen Series? Gracie from Bossy Mr Ward has her own story in The Christmas Agreement. Click Here to read it now.

ALSO BY SHARON WOODS

The Gentlemen Series

Accidental Neighbor

Bossy Mr. Ward

White Empire

The Christmas Agreement

Resisting Chase

The Chicago Billionaire Doctor's Series

Doctor Taylor

Doctor I Do

Doctor Gray